THE PURPLE CHAIR

BOOKS 1 - 6

BRONNIE WARE

ISBN: 978-0-6459351-9-6

Published by Platypus Creek Publishing, Australia.

Adult themes are covered in the book's content.

1

HUMMINGBIRD CAKE

The cushion wrapped up the sides of her bum as she sat heavily into it. Her hands arrived comfortably on the welcoming arms of the chair. Its high back allowed her neck to relax. Staring at the ceiling, she heard the door to the street close down the stairs. A spider wove its secret web in the afternoon light, wrapping around the chandelier above her as it was determined to do each night before the cleaner removed it in the morning. It would have been nice to leave it there. Gwen welcomed the company. Only she and the tiny spider knew all that was shared from this chair. But with phobias and paranoia being just a part of what she listened to each day, she couldn't take the risk. This work was her survival, her income. The web could not stay, but for now she marvelled as the little creature set up again for the evening.

Six clients today, heard and feeling clearer, if only for a little while, until their old stories surfaced again and fought to win. Some would win over their story. The power of the human spirit was remarkable when the pull forward was strong enough. Finding out what that actual pull was for most clients was the hard bit, waiting as they scraped deeper into their wounds and reactions.

Tomorrow was a shorter day. Gwen loved Tuesdays. Always had. It had been a Tuesday when her mother took her out of school to get her ears pierced. She was eight and, as one of seven children, having her mother to herself was a treat indeed. When her mother's face had poked in through the classroom door, she had been confused. Was it good news or bad? But it was simply her mother wanting to do something special just for Gwennie, as she called her.

She'd had a love affair with Tuesdays ever since, and with earrings. Even when her ears became infected from wearing cheap ones her cheap ex had bought her, she had refused to let the holes close. New holes wouldn't connect her to her mum. Tears welled with the longing of missing her.

Breathing deeply, she pushed herself up from the purple chair. Her clinic room was one of her favourite places, but closing its door at the end of the day was also satisfying. The chill of the late afternoon seeped through the door of the shared hallway downstairs. Gwen wrapped her scarf closer and adjusted her hat. Her hand, gloved in hot pink cashmere, turned the knob and the door opened onto the quiet tree-lined avenue outside.

"Another day, another dollar, hey, Gwen?" Bert asked. The predictability of his words made her smile. His hobby shop closed at the same time as her clinic. With her bike parked in the rack out front, it had been over four years of the same question. There was no need to shake up his world with a new response.

"You got it, Bert. You got it." His smile answered her own and he walked up the path past the other closing stores towards the carpark. Gwen unlocked her bike and pedalled off down the gentle slope. She rounded the corner and joined the slightly busier road towards home. Peak hour in Wattledale was not hard riding. The only car horns were usually locals tooting hello and waving as they overtook her in their cars, or tooting hello to other drivers.

Before the door clicked shut to her cosy flat, Claudia was rubbing herself against Gwen's leg. "Hey, girl!" She bent and picked the cat up, ignoring the black fur left on her turquoise trousers. Claudia lifted her white chin for Gwen's touch, massaging paws, also white against the black, into her shoulder. "How are you, darling girl?" Within seconds, the cat had jumped down and was insisting on dinner. Gwen obliged and then tended to her own meal. The microwave pinged and dinner was served. She wished she could find the motivation to prepare healthier meals like she used to.

Monday evenings almost felt like Fridays since Tuesdays were her non-negotiable self-care afternoon, with no work. It was two or three clients, as little paperwork as possible, and out the clinic door by 11 am. Settling into her Monday evening, with her feet up and her finger on the TV's remote control, she was interrupted by the ringing of her phone. She sighed, seeing her brother's name on its screen, and chose the remote instead. She had watched this whole series of *Miranda* before, more than once, but sometimes it was the only thing to make her laugh out loud. It was a *Miranda* sort of night. She chewed on the first bite of tuna mornay, straight from the plastic tray it came in. Every time she ate this meal, she let her mother down, if only in her own eyes. Her mother had taught her how to make the best one on the planet, but four minutes in the microwave with a frozen imitation was so much easier.

Ignoring the calls from Mark, her older brother but not

the oldest, became too hard after four attempts in half an hour. She paused the show.

"Hi, Mark. What's up?"

"Oh, you *are* there? Why did you ignore my calls then?"

"I had stuff to do, no big deal. Like I said, what's up?"

"It's just bloody rude to ignore my call."

Gwen sighed. "What do you want, Mark? If you're just here to hassle me, then I'm hanging up."

"No need to be like that. You're the one who ignored my call."

"Goodbye, Mark."

"Wait! Geez, you're so sensitive. I'm just checking that you're coming to visit Mum on Saturday."

"I'm not sensitive. You're just rude. And yes, of course I am. I don't need you to check. As if I wouldn't be there. I'll see you then."

"Be like that, then. See ya."

"Bye, Mark." She pressed the red button and claimed her evening back.

Raindrops kissed the window gently, leaving winking diamonds when the sun tried to break through.

"She's just awful. That's the simple truth."

"That may well be, Nina, but the question is how you're going to handle this?"

It was Nina's third session in the purple chair. The bright earrings and vivid handbags changed each time, but the clothes, whether a dress or pants and a top, remained consistently black. She exhaled loudly before replying in her thick Spanish accent.

"Well, one thing's for sure – I'm done with being her visitor. And the same for my other siblings. For *years* I've been showing up, asking them about their lives. Showing interest! And what do I get in return? Nada! Not one of them ever asks about me. And then she dares to turn around and treat me like I've got no idea about life when I've done more living than all of them combined!"

Nina's nostrils flared and her jaw clenched as she stared out the window. Gwen sat waiting, allowing the comfortable silence to wrap around them. Its softness slowly seeped into her client's heart.

Nina inhaled deeply, allowing her exhale to fill the space. "I've been thinking about what you said last session, though. How sometimes the only power we have is in how we react. Which I like, even if it's for the wrong reason."

Gwen looked at her client questioningly.

"Well, managing my reaction could bring me peace, perhaps. But I do it because when I don't react it pisses her off more than when I cry or look upset. So I sort of have the upper hand. I win."

The look offered in reply said enough.

"Oh, alright," Nina said. "Am I *really* at peace?"

"That's the question indeed," Gwen said with a smile.

"No, but it's a start – like there's a shift in power between us. I mean, really, we just happened to be born into the same family. The less she affects me, the freer I could be."

"Hypothetically, Nina, yes. But why not let love for yourself pull you forward, rather than your scorn of her? How about we stop focusing on her for today and consider that? What does loving yourself look like, or feel like?"

When people considered this question, tears often

surfaced. Opening to receive their own love was painful for almost every one of her clients. Just considering the possibility triggered a mixture of relief and terror. Some were waiting for someone to give them permission, but that had to come from themselves.

Gwen was not averse to offering a hug on occasion. She had realised a long time ago that hugs sometimes helped her clients more than an hour in the chair, getting lost in the paralysis of verbal analysis. She refused to allow the dryness of her university qualifications to stand in the way of humanity. As a torrent of pain and relief flowed from them, she held them instead of just sitting and watching. Nina's tears dampened the shoulder of her shirt.

On Tuesday, after the morning's work was done, Gwen decided to drive to Kestrel. It was a pretty town, just under an hour's drive from Wattledale, but far enough for her not to be recognised by clients or any friends of her siblings. Light rain reduced her choices of things to do as she pulled up to park on the wide, country street. It didn't bother her. One of Gwen's favourite things was to read a trashy novel with a shockingly predictable ending. She liked to rebel against her usual limit of one ordinary strength coffee per day and drink two strong ones back-to-back. Those coffees, along with reading something so wonderfully shallow, were all she sometimes needed to escape her reality of adult responsibilities. She found the quaint café she had noticed on Instagram and was pleased to see the cakes matched the images her screen had already tantalised her with.

Tuesday afternoons were a time for not really caring – but still caring enough to not sabotage the rest of her week with complete abandon. Such delights reconnected her with an adult version of childish play. It balanced the heaviness of listening to clients all week, too often topped off by the general heaviness of her family. She was dreading Saturday, seeing them all again, but would never miss the day for her mum.

The hummingbird cake was divine. Laden with sugar and spices, not gluten-free, not dairy-free, and enough to fill her up without being so much as to deliver regret. Washing it down with the strong coffee, Gwen smiled at her mutiny. It wasn't much, she knew, but it was absolutely guilt-free. The wellness industry exhausted her at times and while she generally ate well – excluding microwave dinners, hummingbird cake and double-shot coffees – sometimes she wanted to live back in the 1970s and 80s when no one gave a shit about gluten or dairy, not even her.

The wind picked up while she stamped the crumbs of hummingbird cake on the plate under her fingertips and transferred them to her tongue. A paper bag blew past the window, speckled with a few raindrops. She wondered what its story was. What had it held? She imagined putting a tracker inside to find out where it landed but thought the local rubbish dump was most likely and not at all exciting.

She had only taken a few steps outside, the wind reaching her bones under her long coat, when she woke to four people standing over her. She sniffled and blood stained her hand as she wiped under her nose. Confusion rendered speech impossible. She stared at three concerned hovering adult faces and a guilty teenage one, while a pebble on the hard footpath underneath her back edged further into her skin.

"Are you OK? Can you talk?" The panic in the woman's voice scared Gwen almost as much as finding herself in this position.

"Relax, Kath. She's just coming around," the other woman chipped in.

"Oh, I couldn't handle it if she's not OK. You stupid boy." Kath hit what appeared to be her teenage son over the head. "What were you thinking, skating where people are trying to walk?"

The man's gentle voice entered the chaos unfolding above her. "Are you OK? You copped a skateboard in the head as you walked out the café door there. You fell and have been out for about a minute.

Gwen could feel an increasing ache where it had made contact. She sat up, as his arms quickly offered support to ease the move. "Yes, I'm OK. Thank you all."

"Oh, thank God! Thank God!" Kath hit her son across the head again. The boy flinched – from habit rather than surprise.

"Come on, Kath. Let's give the poor dear some space," her friend offered. "You don't think you have a concussion do you, love?"

"No, I'm fine, thanks. Just a bit of a bump, but no hospital needed," Gwen assured them, tenderly touching her head.

"I'm really sorry, lady. It just flipped," the boy said as he was dragged off down the street.

"Here. Let me help you, please," the man offered, pulling her to her feet and then brushing the mop of curls from his face.

"Thanks."

"Are you really OK? I could take you somewhere?"

"No, I'm good, but thank you. Just a little surprised. You

don't generally expect to cop a skateboard in your head on a quiet Tuesday afternoon."

He laughed gently. "No, you don't." Extending his hand he added, "I'm Russell. Russ."

She shook his hand. "Gwen."

"May I buy you a coffee, Gwen?"

"No, but thanks. I think I'll head on home."

"Are you local?"

"Not far away, but not from here."

"OK. Well ... it was good to meet you. You're definitely positive that you're OK?"

She assured him she was and said goodbye, feeling his eyes on her as she left. Another coffee was the last thing she needed. She could only handle so much excitement in one day.

Daniel had been one of Gwen's first clients when she had started up her own clinic. He had been overseas for a few years and now sat back in the purple chair. His cheeks were sunken and a few grey hairs accompanied his return. His smile was still warm when it managed to rise, but his clear blue eyes expressed a sadness that she hadn't witnessed before.

"She wasn't perfect, Gwen. Who of us ever is? But she was to me. She was feisty and challenged me. I liked that. She saw my efforts and acknowledged them. I lifted my game because something about her made me want to."

"You certainly do seem changed, Daniel. Tell me a bit more."

"Well, here's the thing I can't get past: to grow close we had to trust each other. But when you do that, as I did with Alicia, then you land yourself in a pretty vulnerable place, don't you think?"

Gwen nodded and took a sip of her fresh mint tea. Tempted to close her eyes and inhale deeply, she resisted and focused on Daniel. He explained how he had dived fully into raw and honest conversations that had helped them both grow.

"They were exhausting sometimes too – we went deep. It brought us closer, though, and I felt safe in a way I'd never known."

He took a sip from his cup of mint tea. "Now and then I'd get a sense something wasn't right. Like one time when I was talking about getting married and having kids. She'd usually talk about it with me, but this time she was kind of nodding and smiling without actually saying anything." He frowned at the memory and shook his head slowly.

"Then my visa was expiring and I needed her help to stay. We lived together and had a joint bank account. It was all legitimate. But she just started slipping away. It was when she said that the visa process might take longer than she could commit to, I knew it was over. Turns out she was already with someone else by then. I worked it out. Well, I saw them together playing tennis. I sat in the car and watched them, like a damn stalker, and sure enough, the kiss over the net at the end was indeed the end, for me."

"Oh, Daniel, I'm sorry to hear that. What did you do?"

"I packed up everything that day, withdrew my half of the money in the account, and then stayed in a motel for two weeks, while I wound up my work and said goodbye to mates. She didn't even try to contact me. No phone call, nothing. Three years and nothing! What's the point of having the balls to open up when there are no guarantees anyway?"

Gwen sat in silence, allowing it to weave its magic as it always did. Silence had been her own friend growing up. It was her safe place. Most people underestimated its power.

"Oh, I don't know, Gwen," Daniel continued. "I don't want to turn into one of those cynical old blokes who hates women. I just hate myself for being such a dickhead."

"You don't really hate yourself, Daniel. You're just hurting a lot. Let me ask you this. Do you regret it? *Truly* regret it?"

He considered this and then shook his head. "No. It was fabulous for a long time and I learnt a lot. I won't ever regret that. But I feel like there's nothing solid under me anymore. Like I'm floating on a sheet of ice in the ocean, not knowing where it will land or if it will melt first."

"OK. If it melted, who would you depend on to help you survive?"

He stared at the wooden floorboards, darkened from decades of footsteps upon them, then looked at her.

"Me, Gwen. I'd depend on myself, I guess. And right now, I don't think I could stop it from sinking or have the strength to swim." She nodded as he took a deep breath over his cup. "Lovely tea, by the way. Did you grow the mint?"

"Yes." She smiled. "You're hurt, and having to start again, but it doesn't sound like something to regret, even if the end result has broken a part of the old you." She waited for her words to sink in. "And perhaps that was needed to make space for the new parts of yourself to move on in."

"It's so hard imagining them together, though."

"Then don't."

He smiled and nodded. "Yes, I know, I know. I'm not doing myself any favours there."

"One of the only true powers we have, Daniel, ever, is where we direct our thoughts. It's easy to get stuck in old stories and feel sorry for ourselves. We've all been there and it's part of the process of letting go. But how long we stay there determines whether we live a sad or hopeful life."

Daniel nodded.

"Don't deny your sadness or anger," Gwen continued, "but be stronger than them and choose a way forward. Step by step the past will let go a bit until the new reality takes up more of your thoughts than the past. Like I said, it's a process. You don't just wake up there. But your power lies in where you direct your thoughts in the meantime and how long you choose to linger on things that don't bring you joy, or on things that could pull you forward."

Gwen often thought of the seat of the purple chair as the cushion of a thousand sighs. Daniel added one to the tally and smiled.

"Thanks, Gwen. Thanks for asking if I regretted it, because I don't, as raw as it still feels. I still have a way to go, but today has at least been a start."

Gwen sat in the purple chair herself when Daniel had gone. It was a recent habit she had developed when the last client left each day. While they saw her listening ear as their saviour, clients often worked out some of their own solutions. Gwen offered very direct questions and snippets of advice to help them find their way there, but some found their own answers. She sometimes wondered if it was the chair itself. When she was pondering some of her own lessons, the safety of the chair, its purple velvet sides cocooning her, always seemed to take her somewhere better. It had been a wise investment. She added her own sigh to the thousand and one, said goodnight to the little spider, and walked downstairs for her end-of-day greeting from Bert outside his hobby shop.

~

The lump on Gwen's head was still tender after a few days but had reduced in size. It still puzzled her that such a thing had happened, but she was grateful it hadn't been worse. Just weird. She lay on her couch with Claudia curled into her, purring, and flicked through her streaming options and new programs to the services. Ignoring them, she chose *Miranda*, which was sitting in her favourites list. Sometimes there was no better solution than a clever, delightful British sitcom. She was only five minutes into it when her phone rang. Why must they always ring at this time, she asked herself on seeing one of her sisters' names on the screen. She paused the show.

"Hey, Jackie. How're things?"

"I'm so busy. Harold is working all the time and the kids are driving me crazy. Ella's rabbit got out and I think it may have been eaten by the neighbour's dog. She thinks it's run to the grocery store to get a carrot, found some friends and hopped off to visit Peter Rabbit in the forest. Rochelle's determined to wear miniskirts shorter than her belly button and scowls every time she sees me. Surely I wasn't like that as a tween. Was I? No, of course, I wasn't. The twins aren't interested in anything except their screens, which at least brings me some peace, but the other day when Lisa went to the toilet I checked her iPad and she was playing some game about murdering people. Leanda's obsessed with home decorating apps, so I guess that's at least better than murder.

And my legs haven't been shaved in God knows how long, not that I want to look sexy. The last thing I want is for Harold to notice me and want more sex. No, thank you. He gets his 10 minutes' worth twice a week and that's enough. Anyway, enough about me, are you going to see Mum on Saturday?"

"Of course I am. Why is that the only thing anyone asks me?"

"Oooh, touchy, touchy! I was just checking. See you there then. Rochelle!! You are not going out in that. Ella, get out of the fridge. Oh, I have to go. Bye, Gwen." She was gone before Gwen could reply.

∾

Saturday was coming around too fast. Her siblings didn't know she regularly visited their mother alone. It was always much nicer – if you could call it that – without them all there. After browsing her wardrobe for the occasion, Gwen's mood dragged. She had been trying not to buy any clothes for over a year. The fashion industry was a major player in stuffing up the planet and she didn't want to contribute to it. But microwave meals and a slice too many of hummingbird cake meant there was nothing comfortable that she didn't wear to work. Her mother deserved more effort than that. A new dress would also lift Gwen's spirits, she decided. After work on Friday, she headed around the corner from her clinic to the clothing stores.

Being more practical than dreamy, she found the perfect dress in a short time. Bright orange and hot pink, mid-length and flowing, with a collar, funky buttons down the front, and a matching belt with a great 1970s buckle. Her mother loved bright colours and would appreciate the choice. A haircut was overdue so Gwen ducked in to see if her usual stylist could fit her in, apologising for not making an appointment. He was happy to stay back for such a long-term client, as long as he could enjoy a wine in the process.

The sun shone softly the next morning. Magpies gurgled their delightful song from a nearby tree, a sound her mother had loved. Tears arrived instantly. How was she going to handle this with all of them there? She took a deep breath and let it out. All that mattered was for her to show up for her mum and not totally fall apart.

"What on earth are you wearing?" her oldest brother, Carl, asked as she walked across the grass. "Are you going to a freaking *party*?" Gwen ignored him while noting the same look on all her siblings' faces as she approached. None of the six expressed any warmth. Their children were all dressed in black.

"Colours make Mum happy. They always have. I'm dressed for her, not you lot."

She walked past them, refusing to look directly at anyone, and headed straight to the grave. Bending down, she dropped a single pink rose near the headstone and whispered, "Hello, Mummy darling. I love you".

Carl called everyone together and they circled the grave, casting a shadow of gloom. "Right. We're here to visit Mum, who died a year ago today. Is there anything anyone wants to say?"

Faces were turned to the ground. Tears rolled down Gwen's cheeks. She talked to her mother all the time, out loud and silently. There was certainly nothing she needed to say in front of these people, all of whom had either ignored their mother or bullied her as soon as they were old enough to.

"Happy anniversary, Mum," Jackie said. *Happy anniversary! Oh man,* Gwen thought. *The woman waits on you and your kids hand and foot and that's all you come up with. You think she wants to hear a happy anniversary to celebrate that she's dead? Can't wait for the next one.*

"I hope you're OK, Mum," one of her younger brothers offered. *You hope she's OK? She's dead, you idiot, and she died without any of you having the balls to visit her in her last twelve months, just because she'd had a breakdown. Keep going, you lot, let's hear the next one.*

"Bye, Nan," Rochelle said. *I guess that'll do, though I'm sure she would have preferred you'd said hello in person when she was still actually alive.*

"Thanks for being a good cook," Petra, Gwen's younger sister, said. "I loved your caramel slice." *Good point.*

It seemed the circle of greetings was coming around and Gwen wouldn't be able to abstain.

"I hope you're OK wherever you are," her other younger brother said. *Me too, Mum, me too.*

"You did a good job raising everyone," her niece announced. *Really? She certainly tried, but the results aren't in.*

"Thanks for all the birthday money, Nan." *Hmm, and the love?*

It was Gwen's turn. Instead of staring at the grave as they had for each other, they now turned to look at her. *Stuff them,* she thought, *this is for Mum.* "Beautiful Mum," she said, "I miss you every day. I miss your laugh, your understanding, your kindness, and your delight in the simplest things. I miss everything about you." Tears poured down her cheeks and her nose dripped. "I miss shopping with you, cooking with you, walking with you, and just hanging around at home with you. A year's gone by so fast and I miss you just as much every day. Oh Mum, thank you so much for the love you gave. I hope—"

"Right," Carl interrupted. "Anyone else? We haven't got all day."

"Bye, Mum."

"Bye, Nan."

"Yeah, bye, Mum." A few more mumbles of goodbye came from siblings, their partners and children.

"Right. See you all next year, then," Carl announced. "Just look for the clown clothes on Gwen and you'll find the grave." Chuckles rang through the tribe and they dispersed, leaving only the loving clown standing at the grave.

Touching the tombstone gently, Gwen said goodbye to her mother. An incredible woman who no one had ever seemed to see, except for her. *Their loss*, she told herself, but it was her loss that tore her apart. "Oh, Mum," she whispered.

She needed some recklessness. Scream to the open sky or eat cake? she asked herself. Both? But there was no scream to be found. She found herself heading to the café in Kestrel, the one with the hummingbird cake. She always tried to vary her cake exploration, but this wasn't Tuesday. There were no rules in place for Saturdays or the anniversary of a mother's death.

With no trashy novel in the car, she ventured to the newsagent and flicked through the magazines. Why would she want to read gossip about anyone, let alone people she had never met? No amount of sadness could make her desperate enough for those magazines. A wellness one? she asked herself. *No, too many perfect people talking about kale.* House decorating magazines? *No, I like my home as it is.* Horse magazines, cat ones, cars? *I don't think so.* Naked women? *It doesn't do much for me.* Cooking? *Too many memories of Mum.* Travel? *Yes, perfect! It'll take me away from myself, at least for the duration of two cups of coffee.*

"Gwen!"

She looked up from fumbling for her purse in her large handbag.

"Oh, Russ ... ell, Russ. Do you work here?"

"Yes, I own this shop."

"I had no idea." She handed over the money for the magazine.

"How's your head?"

"Oh!" She had forgotten that with the headache of family. "It's fine, thank you."

"Are you hanging around? May I buy you that coffee I offered the other day? My staff can hold the fort here for a while?"

Escapism. She had asked for it. Anything to take her out of herself.

"Uh, OK, thanks. Why not?"

∼

Her light green work pants, with the coloured trim around the hem, blended well with the purple chair. The cream top with flowing sleeves went with almost anything.

Well done, Gwennie, her mother would have laughed, *even matching your clothes to your furniture.*

The grief came in waves. It never subsided completely, but sometimes the shock of never seeing her mother again crippled her. She might be paying for petrol and the world would suddenly swirl. She didn't want to remember her new reality.

She couldn't afford this loss of clarity at the start of her working day. *Walk your talk, Gwen, my dear: focus on something more hopeful or positive.*

The cleaner had been in near dawn. No spider web hung on the chandelier. She hoped the spider had a full belly from its evening's work. She had never sat in the chair in the morning light, a realisation she found both astonishing and entertaining. Some of her clients only visited in the mornings and others in the afternoons. She considered how differently the rays might affect them. She stood up, banged on her lower back with her fists to awaken her kidneys – at least according to her online Qi Gong instructor – and welcomed her first client of the day into the room.

"The thing is," Amara explained, running fingers through her afro hair, "I didn't really want to be a mother, but here I am doing it with my dropkick husband. Actually, he's not that bad, just a bit placid, I suppose. But we have nothing in common. We never did. It was an arranged marriage, you see. We just parent our three teenagers together, and I've spent most of their life counting down to their departure. People say it goes so fast, but I think it *drags*. I'm there for them. I listen to them. I hug them. I try to believe in them. But I wish they'd just hurry up and leave so I can have my life back."

"What's the life you want back?" Gwen asked. "Do you think it still exists, or is it a new life you're dreaming of?"

"I don't know. I guess I just want to feel less responsibility." Amara briefly screwed her lips up in thought. "I just want to be Amara for a while, like having time to play my banjo and get some real rhythm going without being interrupted. That'd be a change! And being able to say yes to lunch with friends without having to watch the clock for the school run. I want to be able to walk around my house naked without the husband taking it as an invitation for sex or the kids being embarrassed and telling me to put some clothes on."

"Have you had a holiday without them all, or even just a couple of days to yourself, in the last few years?"

"I sure have. I had four days away at the coast by myself last year. There was a moment, a couple of days in, when I'd cooked some malva pudding and eaten the whole lot without having to share it, that I did miss them. For a moment. But then I stayed up until 3 am watching movies because I didn't have to get up for anyone. It was wonderful! Then I started to dread going back. I returned worse than when I left. It's too tantalising. I really don't think I can do that again."

"It sounds like there are some important needs of your own not being met, Amara. Perhaps if we have a look at that, you might find a way to honour yourself within your current life."

Amara sighed. "I *would* actually like to be more present for them. I'll probably leave the husband when they leave. Or maybe not. Maybe I'll realise that he's a good and steady man who I do love in some weird manner. But either way, the youngest is only thirteen so I have at least five years left. That's a *long* time. At least the oldest will be finishing school next year, so that'll shift things, maybe give me a bit more time. I hope so, anyway."

Gwen suggested that they make a list of things that Amara imagined for her life of freedom, so she could start incorporating some of that into her current life.

"Maybe, Gwen. I'd rather be hopeful than cynical. They're good kids. They deserve to be appreciated, not just resented. But five years still feels like *forever*."

"That's why we need to work on a solution. You deserve to find some happiness through these years too, you know?"

Amara nodded and rose. "Happiness. Yes." She looked wistfully around the room until her eyes landed back on the chair she had been sitting in. "I like your chair, by the way. This space is really welcoming, and the colourful pots with the plants brighten the place up. You could be an interior designer, or a fashion stylist."

"I might not meet good people like you if I was either of those, Amara. Now please, come sit down. Let's work on that list of how to make some small changes to support yourself."

Amara reached for her woven bag instead and swung it over her shoulder. "I'm not ready for this stuff yet, Gwen, but thanks. I'm not a middle way sort of person. I'm more of an all-or-nothing."

"But what if that's not making you happy?"

"Happy. There's that word again. Maybe I'm not to know happiness."

"Peace, perhaps?"

"Oh, I'm definitely not to know that one." Sadness flitted across her face and was gone.

"I'd like to help you, Amara. Small changes *can* lead to lasting change."

Amara looked at Gwen a moment and then shook her head. "No. I don't actually think anything can help me now." She opened the door.

"You deserve happiness."

"So you say, Gwen. Look, I *will* come back. I've just realised that I'm not quite ready yet. Thanks anyway." Amara pulled the door closed as Gwen uttered a rushed farewell. She knew she couldn't save everyone, but her heart was still left heavy with sadness.

~

A sudden urge to cook found Gwen poring through her recipes on Friday evening after work. Frustrated with the lack of inspiration, she scrolled for recipes on her phone then opened one of the two cookbooks she had pilfered from her mother's belongings.

It had been obvious her mother would not be coming home from the care home after her breakdown. The house had stood empty for months. Gwen had watered the plants right up until the day it was sold. Knowing her siblings and their lack of respect for anything of sentimental value, accompanied by their greed for anything of monetary worth, she had claimed what she could. She had taken a few things that would keep her mother alive in her heart, personal things of no value to anyone else: two cookbooks, her mother's favourite brooch, birthday cards she had kept from Gwen, the rare photo of her mother as a child, and a small scrapbook of pictures from magazines that became a story of unfulfilled dreams.

The nursing home had offered her the nightdress her mother had died in. She had declined. It only reminded her of a desperate woman walking barefoot down an icy street, not knowing her own name, or much at all, only that she wanted out of the almost-caged existence she had ended up in. When they found her, frozen and dead, curled up under the pine tree on the edge of town, Gwen knew she had been heading to a special place under a particular willow tree. It was a place of memories for her mother as a young woman. It had also become a special place for mother and daughter, with secret picnics as adults, sharing stories never told to others. She hadn't been there in the year since her mother died, but hoped that one day she would be brave enough for the pain and joy of it.

Her heart ached to see her mother's handwritten notes altering some of the recipes. Claudia jumped onto the bench, sitting beside the open book.

"Get down, you cheeky girl. You know you're not allowed up here!" As she went to lift the cat down, Claudia hissed and sat on the open page of the second book lying nearby. "Oh, you want me to cook this recipe, do you?" Gwen lifted her up and smiled. "Tuna mornay, of course." The cat was then willing to be placed back on the floor. "Tuna mornay, hey, Mum? I know, I know. I'll give up the frozen version, I promise, and do you justice." She read through the ingredients and committed them to memory. She put on her coat and headed out to the store.

The smell of home cooking floated through her home a little later. It nurtured Gwen's heart in a way she hadn't known she needed. The last rays of winter sunshine fell upon the birdbath in her little courtyard. She sat inside at the small, square table by the window and took a bite as a few tears fell. Her mother would be proud. It was scrumptious.

2

THE LISTENER

White synthetic fluff stuck to the purple velvet. Gwen picked the tiny pieces from the cushion meticulously and emptied them into the bin. Her client, Maxine, a lanky woman with olive skin and bright orange-dyed hair, always seemed to leave a sign of her presence behind in the clinic room. Marvelling at the huge range of personalities across her clients, Gwen reminded herself that it was a sample of all of humanity. While many tried to do what was expected, behave themselves and live "normal" lives, she had worked out a long time ago that there was actually no such thing as normal.

Her rumbling belly reminded her it was lunchtime. She grabbed her funky coat, bottle green with gold thread outlining flowers of all colours, and headed down the stairs onto the street. A recent revival of home cooking was bringing her much pleasure in the evenings, but today's lunch would be takeaway. She told herself that once the days warmed up, with spring not too far off, she would bring leftovers and eat them down the road at the park. For now, it was still a bit chilly to be eating outdoors.

"Hi, Auntie Gwen," her niece Samantha said. "Here, take this table." It was unfortunate that her brother's daughter chose to work at the café in town she really loved. Sometimes Gwen gave her business to a different one, just to avoid giving her niece any fodder for the family to gossip about.

"Nice coat. Are you going to a fancy dress party?"

"No, Samantha. I'm leading a runway fashion show for creative psychologists. All I need are some orange boots with purple spots and I'm ready to roll!"

Samantha laughed. "OK, I asked for that. Sorry. What would you like for lunch?"

Gwen turned her focus to the menu, though she knew it by heart. She ordered the roast vegetable and herb soup with a fresh bread roll.

As soon as it arrived and wafted under her nostrils, she knew it was the perfect choice for a day of low temperatures.

"Auntie Gwen?"

She looked up, licking soup from her lip. "Yes, Samantha. What is it this time?" she asked mildly. "You don't like my necklace either?"

Samantha shook her head. "I like your necklace, a lot actually. Your jacket too, if I'm really honest. I just wanted to say again that I'm sorry. I'm so used to mocking you. It's ... what my family does. But—" her niece's voice quivered. Gwen waited while Samantha gulped, took a deep breath, and tried again.

"I'm sorry, Auntie Gwen. I actually really admire you. The way you hold your own in such a messed-up family. I'd like to get to know you more, if you're willing. But I'm scared of being mocked, just by being associated with you."

Gwen let the declaration sink in for a moment then smiled gently. "I understand that, Samantha. It can take some courage to go against your family, but there's a lot of freedom in it too."

Her niece nodded in relief. "Then we can hang out sometime?"

"I reckon we can, sweetheart. We can also keep it quiet if you need to."

As Gwen was leaving, Samantha rushed over and threw a hug around her. A little at a loss for words, Gwen fought back her own tears and whispered, "See you soon" into her niece's hair before leaving without looking back.

She took a detour back to the clinic, absorbing the incident. Not much in life surprised Gwen anymore, but it was certainly a nice twist in her day.

Heading back up the stairs, she smiled at her sign on the door. Despite her qualifications as a psychologist and counsellor, she had chosen the title "Listener". What she hadn't factored in was how many clients it would attract, including many who would never have gone to someone with her formal titles.

Gwen recalled her mother's delight when she had told her of her plans. She choked down the tears that threatened to surface, remembering her mother's hands clapping and her feet bouncing in enthusiasm. The ache in Gwen's heart had barely eased in over a year. How could it be that the one person in the world who understood her was no longer even in it? She thought of the saying "We are never given more than we can handle" and wished she could know who first said it so she could go and punch them in the head. How could life go on without her dear mother being in it?

~

Gwen had agreed to meet her client Gladys at the bottom of the stairs. The old building had a lift, down the hall at the back. She guided Gladys there, rather than watch the 93-year-old try to climb the stairs. Once up in the clinic and comfortable in the purple chair, Gladys looked around the clinic room. Her grey hair was perfectly rolled into hidden clips. Her navy shoes matched her handbag, which sat in her lap as she turned to Gwen with a smile of approval. She breathed in deeply and remarked, "It even smells lovely. Is that a lemongrass candle you have burning?"

"Yes. A nice candle can make such a difference to a space, I find. Now, may I make you a cup of tea before we dive in? I have fresh mint or regular black tea?"

"Oh no, thank you, darling. Water is just fine."

Gwen sat the drink beside her, sat herself down, and asked her to share what was bothering her.

"Oh, this is so strange, pouring out my woes to a pretty young thing like you. But they said you're good at this. I think it might be me who isn't."

"Take your time, Gladys."

"It's my daughter who wanted me to come. She's seventy, you know, not a spring chicken herself. She says I need to work on my 'inner child'. I have no idea what that even means. She described it as being the little girl who still lives inside of me, but I can hardly even remember being a little girl. It was a long time ago, darling." Gladys smoothed down the velvet on the chair's arm.

"What does she think the problem is? It must be compelling for you to have landed here."

"I'm not saying I agree with her," Gladys said, "but she says I wasn't really there for her as a parent." The elderly woman paused, looked at the floor, and grew sombre. Then she glanced up again. "I didn't work outside the home. I met my daughter at the door after school with freshly baked biscuits or cakes almost every day. I made her clothes, grew vegetables and fed her, sat with her through her homework. My goodness, darling, these accusations coming at me at ninety-three have been a bit of a shock, I must say. I certainly gave her a better childhood than I had."

"Tell me about that, Gladys."

"Oh, there's not much to tell. I was born during the Depression. My parents were in survival mode. Their love was practical. It had to be, just to keep us alive. There was no time for fluffing around with crying children. You learnt not to complain, to pitch in with the jobs, and be grateful for any food on the table. And there always was. It may have only been two potatoes some nights, but we were always fed. I knew how to darn my socks and milk a cow by the time I was three."

"Yes, a different era entirely," Gwen commented.

"That's right, but now my daughter says I'm unemotional. Heavens, darling, I've raised eight children. My husband died young, working with asbestos. We didn't know about the danger of it back then. I did my best. I do think my daughter needs to forgive my lack of hugs. I was in survival mode myself."

"Have you explained all this to her?"

"No," Gladys admitted. "I'd never really thought about my childhood that way. But sitting in this lovely chair with a complete lack of judgement on your sweet face, I can see it. She's probably right in that the little girl I was didn't get enough love. But none of us did. It was just how it was. So I do think, with that considered, I've done a rather remarkable job of parenting."

"Do you think you could share this with your daughter? It may help her understand ... or not. But at least you could try."

Gladys pushed herself up to stand. "I believe I can try, darling. I may see you again to talk to this little girl in me, but probably not. You've already helped me more than you know. Thank you."

Gwen reminded Gladys that she still had more time left if there was anything more that she needed to talk about, but she was waved off with a smile. It was the same when she offered to escort the old woman to the lift. She watched as Gladys ambled to it and disappeared behind its closing doors.

Gwen sat down in the purple chair. It was often not a straightforward solution that left her clients more peaceful. Sometimes it was just having a safe space to speak their thoughts out loud. Having a fixed expectation could rob the session of its potential – as it could with life in general.

∽

"What should I do tomorrow, Claudia?" The cat looked at her mildly and settled back to sleep on the cushion by the window, bathed in the golden glow of the late afternoon.

Every Tuesday Gwen worked a shorter day to enjoy some mid-week hours off, indulging in whatever form of self-care her heart asked for, within reason. Sometimes her Tuesday ideas jostled with each other for her attention. Other times, like this week, there was nothing, no inspiration at all. This lack of inspiration wasn't confined to

Monday nights – she had felt this numbness often since losing her mother.

The phone, its ringer still turned off from work but vibrating on the kitchen bench, brought her out of herself. She wanted to ignore it, but that would create a leak in her energy for the rest of her night.

"Yes, Carl?" It was her oldest brother.

"What? Not even hello?"

"Hello then. What do you want?"

He huffed before replying, "I was ringing to invite you to Simon's 21st birthday party this weekend, but if you're going to be like that, I won't bother."

Heaviness sat upon her heart. She couldn't reply.

"Well?"

"Well what, Carl? Are you inviting me or not, because I don't have time for this nonsense." She had to trust the dread building at the thought of being there. "Anyway, when is it? I have some weekend plans and you're not giving me much notice."

"Too busy for your own nephew's 21st birthday? Stuff you then. I won't bother inviting you."

She stared out the window, straining in the dusk light to see if that was indeed the first minuscule flash of lime green on the bare branch, announcing the turning of the seasons.

"Goodbye, Carl," Gwen said simply and hit the red button. Before she had reached the door to investigate, he was calling back. She ignored it.

With no idea how to spend her precious Tuesday afternoon off, Gwen chose to drive. The chilly wind blew in through the open windows. Music from her phone shouted out through the speakers. She wished there was a good old-fashioned record shop in the area to browse through, but they had long lost their business to online streaming. She would have loved even better to hear some live music, but this wasn't Berlin or New York, or Sydney or London. There was no live music on a Tuesday afternoon in her region.

Her main relationship with Pebbly Creek, the town she drove into, was memories of playing netball there decades ago. Another vague memory of accompanying her mother in the middle of a winter's night to pick up one of her drunk brothers came to mind. Turning off her music she slowed as she turned onto the wide main street. *May as well stop and have a look*, she thought. *There might be a good coffee to be found.* Gwen had learnt that if the cakes on display in any shop were average, the coffee would be too. After walking two blocks, which was almost the entire town, and seeing nothing beyond average, she considered driving on. A distant sound of someone singing caught her ear.

Following the sound, she turned a corner. The music grew clearer. She spotted a guy sitting on a tree stump by his camper van, playing the guitar and singing, down by the small river with his back to the town. She sat a little further up the bank and listened. His voice. Oh my, she thought. Melodic, pure, too good for this town. It deserved to be on stage. She lay back on the grass, hands behind her head, and observed the bare branches above her swaying slightly against the pure blue sky. She closed her eyes and listened to his music. This was better than any record store.

Gwen didn't know the songs and guessed they were originals. Wise, funny, heartbreaking. She listened to five right through, eyes closed. When the sixth one seemed a long time coming, and a shadow crossed her closed eyelids, she opened them to find him standing over her.

"Oh, hello," she said, as though they knew each other.

"Hi. How long have you been here?"

"Since the one about you driving into the city and wanting to get back to the open road." She sat up.

"Oh. That's a while back." He sat beside her. "You shouldn't sneak up on people, you know."

"I didn't," Gwen said. "I was resting here quietly, minding my own business, listening to some songs on the wind. You're the one who snuck up on me."

"Touché. You got me there. I'm Liam."

She shook his extended hand. "Gwen."

"Fancy a coffee, Gwen? I've got my own percolator. Can't trust every country town to have decent coffee."

"Oh, I love you already," she laughed.

They fell into the easy groove of travellers who like each other but know they'll never meet again. She remembered that freedom of her backpacking years as a younger adult, not caring what day of the week it was, doing random things while the world carried on with its routines. Liam spoke of his music. She spoke of her work. He spoke of his future travels. She spoke of her past ones. He spoke of the dog he had recently lost. She spoke of Claudia, her cat.

It went unsaid that they would make love. With the coffee finished and the stories told, the gentle transition into nakedness was natural.

He offered another coffee afterwards, followed by dinner, both of which she declined. Life had given them an afternoon of music and pleasure. She wasn't willing to ruin the gift.

"Play me up the street, will you, please, Liam?" she asked, kissing him goodbye. "Let me hear your music until it fades out of my ears' reach. Then it'll be in my head as I drive home."

"Happy to oblige," he whispered into her hair as they hugged. "Go well, gorgeous lady. It was a pleasure."

"For me too. Travel safe, you." They smiled as lovers before she turned and headed back up the bank onto the footpath beyond. The song was a happy one, ringing out over a mundane conversation she heard along the way. By the time she turned the corner, it was gone, lost in the breeze and distance.

In a quick sweep as he gathered his thoughts, Gwen noticed Haruto's fashionable jeans and the stylish shoes, recently polished. His hair was cut in a trendy style and recently combed, and his jumper was free of even one ball of fluff.

"Is it wrong to be glad your parents are dead?" he asked, fiddling with the silver bracelet he wore. The morning sunlight filtered gently into the clinic, landing on a healthy plant sitting in a blue and white striped pot. She smiled kindly.

"Who's to say what's right and wrong?"

"Great, thanks, because I am. I *am* glad, Gwen. I'm thirty-five years old and I can finally breathe." He let go of the bracelet.

Haruto's older sister by eighteen years had died in a rock-climbing accident before he was born. His parents had him soon after, to replace her.

"What a burden," he said, "to live up to that dream of

theirs. All my life I've felt the weight of that responsibility, to fill their broken hearts and be the perfect son. There've been times I wished they didn't have me, yet here I am. But they were so protective! I felt like I couldn't breathe!"

Gwen could only imagine how stifling that would be.

"It's weird," Haruto continued, playing with his bracelet again. "Because in one way it *was* over the top. Like, don't do that! Be careful! Oh no, that's too dangerous! That sort of thing. And in another way, they weren't there for me at all. So I got all this attention, but at the same time they just weren't there. It was like they were shells, empty – and they didn't see *me* at all."

Gwen watched him sip his mint tea and then took a sip of her own. Dust particles caught in the sunlight. She returned her focus to her client.

"And now they're with her," he said, "if you believe in that sort of thing. It doesn't matter either way. I can breathe, but a part of me feels ashamed that I'm relieved they died in that car crash."

"Do you *really* feel ashamed or do you just think you *should* feel that way?" Gwen prompted.

"Good question. Well, since you're legally obliged to keep this conversation to yourself ... right?"

"Absolutely."

"Then, yes, perhaps I just *think* I should feel guilty or ashamed. I hope they didn't suffer in the end, of course, but it couldn't have been much worse than the suffering they were addicted to their whole lives. I don't think they ever sought help. If I brought it up, they'd change the subject to the price of tomatoes or something."

"Yes. Some people are just too terrified to go there at all."

"I get that, Gwen, and I could almost feel sorry for them, except I had to pay the price for that my whole life."

She allowed the silence to settle. It filtered through the room, allowing them to breathe it in.

"Truth be told, I'm feeling incredibly free. I didn't even know my sister, but I almost hated her for a while. Though I know none of it was her fault." He paused and frowned, looking at Gwen. "Do you think I'm a bad person?"

"Do you?" she asked.

"No. I know how hard I tried to meet their expectations. I loved them as much as they'd let me. But no, I think I'm a pretty good person."

"There's your answer, Haruto. I'll never judge you either way, but you're definitely not a bad person just for being honest with yourself and me. I get it."

His position shifted, indicating a willingness to wind up the session.

"So what does this life of freedom to be yourself look like?" she asked.

"I don't know yet. I could even come out and live honestly as the gay man I am. I don't know. I'm still working out what freedom means to me." He stood and reached out his hand in farewell.

She shook it and said, "Let me know if I can help you work through that, Haruto."

"Thank you, Gwen. I think I might. It would be new territory to live openly, on top of everything else. I've suffered all my life, thinking I'm not enough, and it's time I realised I am."

She smiled warmly.

"I can't thank you enough," he said. "Your reputation preceded you and I get why. Thanks, Gwen."

"My pleasure, Haruto. Good luck."

"Actually, can we book another appointment now, in a while. Give me a little time to adjust first?"

Together they found an agreeable time two months away.

Haruto's footsteps seemed a little lighter to her ear than when he had trudged in. The door closed and Gwen moved to sit in the purple chair. It was a memory of her mother that woke her from the brief snooze. She tried to grasp it, to hold onto the sound of her voice, but it was gone.

～

Gwen had been born smack bang in the middle of a very balanced birthing order. There were two older brothers and an older sister, and two younger brothers and a younger sister. Her siblings weren't all best friends with each other, but their drinking and similar lifestyles meant they could at least pretend sometimes. Gwen, on the other hand, had long given up pretence in any form. Such independence sat uncomfortably with them.

It was Timothy on the phone this time, the younger brother closest to her age. "Come on, Gwen. Why can't you come to Simon's 21st? It'll be fun."

"Oh, Timothy. You and I both know that your version of fun and mine are two very different things. I have nothing in common with any of you now that Mum is gone."

"That doesn't matter. Just come for a few hours?"

"No, Timothy. Whether I go for 10 minutes or a few hours, it will be too long for me and not long enough for Carl. You'll all find something to mock me for, as usual, no matter which way I go. I don't need to put myself in those situations anymore just to keep the peace for Mum."

"Why do you have to cause so much trouble, Gwen?

Why can't you just say OK, turn up with a smile, and have a good time? Why are you always the one to rock the boat?"

She walked outside into the courtyard, looked up at the cloudy sky, and breathed deeply. "Perhaps I'm not the one rocking the boat, Timothy. Maybe it's all of you, or maybe I'm just happier sailing in a different one."

Gwen felt the shift in mood before her brother's tone confirmed it. "You're such a selfish cow, Gwen. What's more important than your nephew's 21st?"

She counted things off silently on her fingers. *Cutting my toenails. Scrubbing the toilet with a toothbrush. Curling up with my cat...*

"Are you there?"

"Oh! Yes, Timothy, I am, but I'm going now."

"God, you're selfish."

She didn't bother saying goodbye, just hit the red button to end the call.

The next afternoon, Gwen's head was full of client stories. She took a longer-than-usual bike ride home to clear it. The air was crisp with the tease of spring as the days lengthened. She stopped by some public gardens and delighted in the tiny shoots finding their way back from the depths of winter. Migratory birds were starting to return and their songs offered hope.

The willow tree she used to picnic under with her mother might be getting its leaves back too, she thought. Gwen loved the fresh green shades that only early spring could deliver and saw dots of it everywhere, not discernible to a casual glance, but visible everywhere if you really looked. It was time to visit the willow tree. The year of avoidance and self-protection had buffered her pain long enough. Her mother was dead; she was beginning to accept that fact. Gwen knew she had to be brave and go there.

Riding out of town, with the river beside her, she could almost see her mother's brightly coloured dress swishing in the breeze as she waited for Gwen's arrival. The mirage disintegrated, leaving only the swaying branches up ahead.

The tiniest touch of green had returned, as she had hoped, but other than being down a steep bank, the tree offered no privacy. Not like when her mother and Gwen used to picnic there unseen for hours, hidden by the cave of branches, drooping with walls of twisted leaves. Those walls also protected her mother when the world had become too much and the tree became her haven.

Gwen lay her bike on the grass, pushed the branches aside and climbed into the tree's skeletal frame. She could almost remember the sound of her mother crying and how Gwen's heart had ached, holding her, not knowing what else to do. It was under this tree that she had also recognised the gift to others of having a willing listener.

Her mother would sometimes bake a special cake that only they shared. They both enjoyed the secrecy and naughtiness of it, hidden behind the thick veil of branches and leaves. Once they had laid back and laughed so much that their faces ached and Gwen had almost choked.

The smell of the dampness from the river's edge not far below, accompanied by the tree's natural scent, triggered memories. They jostled for attention, blurring into a collage of emotions. The bittersweetness was raw and healthy. Bare branches with their tiny dots of returning green wept with her, too barren to envelop her fully in their protection. She leant against the trunk of the tree, watched the frigid water meander by, and allowed her tears to flow. Gwen cried her own river, supported by the tree, swimming in the memories.

~

The coast seemed like a good idea, rather than running the risk of crossing paths with family on the weekend of her nephew's 21st birthday celebrations. She arrived around 9 pm, having fed Claudia for the night and arranged with a neighbour to feed her for the next. As she drove down the hill into the coastal town of Watkins Beach, the salty air was thick with humidity.

The roar of the ocean, and the breeze skimming across it, woke her senses fully when she opened the balcony door of her hotel room and looked out into the night. Salty air wrapped heavily around her. She breathed it in and felt better immediately.

She rose just before sunrise and walked the resort's path down to the beach. Shadows of other early risers walked before her, their feet meeting the lapping of the new day's waves. Throughout the long walk down to the headland and back, with the light increasing by the minute, her skin felt alive. Kisses from the ocean swished around her ankles.

By the time she had returned to the hotel, the day had fully begun. People were out and about, and the sun was higher, brushing away any remnants of the cool night. The sub-tropical gardens of the resort were covered in colourful flowers against the lushness of their green hues. Gwen loved it all.

There was a salad bar in the town that she had visited a couple of years earlier. Relieved to see it still there, she filled up on a fruit smoothie for breakfast and then bought a few salads to mix for later. She had just returned them to her room's refrigerator and was about to head out to wherever her feet or car decided to take her when she heard a semi-familiar voice. She pulled her door closed and looked up the corridor.

"Gwen? My goodness, what are you doing in Watkins Beach?"

"Russ. Gosh. Can't a girl have any secrets?"

Russ was a new acquaintance, brought into her life unexpectedly when she had been in his town. He had shown kindness when she had taken a fall.

"I'm sorry, I didn't mean to pry. I'm just surprised to see you."

"Well, it's not a brothel or an adult hotel. It's a rather flashy beachside hotel, so why the surprise?" she joked.

He laughed. "Both of us being far from home, that's all. It's great to see you. How are you? What brings you here, or do I even want to know?" He gestured, enquiring whether someone waited in Gwen's room for her.

"I'm doing pretty well, Russ. Here on my own." She smiled. "I just felt like a change of scene and here I am. You?"

"There was a retail expo on here yesterday so I decided to stay on and enjoy an extra day away from the shop. I don't suppose you'd like to join me up on the headland to spot some whales? They're heading back down south to Antarctica. I'm going to drive to the best viewing spot to save some walking time – I have to head home this afternoon."

Gwen thought for a moment but found no reason not to. "OK, why not?"

"Wonderful! You can't deny that life keeps crossing our paths, now, can you?"

She laughed. "Perhaps we'll be friends after all, Russ." He bent his elbow to escort her. She linked her hand with his arm as they walked down the hotel's corridor and out into the sunshine towards his car.

~

Keith manoeuvred his weighty backside into the purple chair, disgust written all over his round, red face.

Gwen's opening questions varied. Sometimes she didn't ask any – the client just started talking. She was about to ask a question then decided to wait and let the silence crack him open.

"I don't even know what I'm doing here. My sister reckons I have control issues and that if I could let go a bit, I might be happier."

"Do you think you have?"

"No, not at all. You're just as bad as her."

Ooh, personal attack, straight into it. Keep going mate and you're out of here.

"And how is that, Keith?"

"A bloody woman who thinks she knows everything."

"And you don't think you know everything?"

"I know a hell of a lot more than you."

Gwen sat quietly, unresponsive.

"My sister reckons my wife left me because I tried to control her."

"Did you?"

"No! Of course not. I provided the money so I got to set the rules of the house."

"Hmm, doesn't sound like too much of an equal relationship, Keith."

"She just stayed home and looked after the kids. God knows what else she did with her time. So if I wanted dinner on the table at 6.30 pm sharp, there shouldn't have been a problem with that. It was the least she could do."

"Well, clearly, it wasn't the least. She also left you."

"I don't need this."

Gwen shrugged and nodded towards the door. Keith stood, red in the face, charged with venom, then sat again, but still looking daggers at her. Gwen looked out the window and waited. One full minute passed, then another.

"What am I supposed to do here?" he asked, a little more mildly. "I've never talked to anyone about this stuff, let alone a woman."

"The first thing you have to do, if you'd like to continue this session, is to ditch the misogynistic comments," Gwen said. "I'm not here to listen to you insulting women. I can handle a lot, Keith, but I also won't tolerate you taking personal aim at me – though your criticism says a lot more about you than me, in any case."

He looked at her. "What's that supposed to mean?"

"Criticism often says much more about the person speaking than the one receiving."

Keith frowned, but remained silent. Gwen waited another minute and then decided on a more compassionate approach.

"So it must have been a shock to come home to an empty house, with no direct warning?"

"Yeah, it was shit. I don't really blame her, though."

With Keith's defences lowered, the session unfolded.

Gwen continued her gentle questions and he answered with less resistance.

He shook her hand in thanks at the end.

"I almost wish I'd never opened this can of worms. I get the feeling it's going to take more than one session to sort this out."

"It's up to you, Keith. I'm here if you need me. Just don't forget that the end goal is more peace for you, and more enjoyment of life for you and everyone you interact with. It might be hard at times, but it's all towards a happier life."

He nodded with a sad smile, tears brimming. "I know."

When she closed the door after him, Gwen was reminded of the power of compassion. Nothing said to her in the clinic was personal. She was her clients' safe place to let go, and they paid her well for it. Still, she didn't deny that the turnaround in that session was a relief, and a job well done.

Samantha, her niece and a young woman now, didn't waste time following up the conversation they'd had at the café. Via text, she asked when Gwen was free. It turned out that Samantha enjoyed bike riding, something Gwen hadn't realised. With drinks and a small lunch in each of their backpacks, they headed south-east, where the sky opened up sooner than in other directions. There was also a small lake on that side of town.

They didn't chat much on the ride, paying close attention to the potholes and passing traffic. Once at the lake, with the bikes parked in the rack provided, they sat at a picnic table, side by side, looking out at the water and the birdlife that called it home.

Samantha asked a lot of questions – about Gwen's life now; about growing up in such a tough family; why her grandfather, Gwen's father, had left her nan; and why her nan, Gwen's mother, was crazy.

"Your nan was far from crazy, Samantha. She was intelligent, kind, supportive and funny. I miss her dearly. She was the best mother anyone could hope for."

Gwen explained that her mother had raised seven of her own children and had then helped raise a number of the grandchildren too. She had been a committed wife from the old generation, where mothers were expected to keep the house and family, while the father went off to work. Gwen's mother had lived for her family, including her grouchy husband, who had never showed her affection.

"But my father speaks about her so differently."

"Yes, well, your father learned to treat her as badly as his father did. I remember listening through cracks in many doors as a child. He was verbally cruel to her, incredibly nasty. I reckon it would've taken a lot of strength to still think well of yourself after decades of that."

Samantha shook her head. "I never knew, Auntie Gwen. I thought she was an idiot because that's what I was told."

"I know, sweetheart, but your nan was definitely not an idiot."

"So why did she end up in the loony bin?"

"Samantha. Please don't ever call it that again."

Shamed, her niece looked down and nodded.

"Your grandfather left your nan out of the blue for a much younger woman. They'd been married for nearly thirty years. All she knew was being his wife. When he left, she didn't know who she was any more. It didn't help that he'd gradually turned most of his kids against her over the years. We were teenagers and young adults by the time he left. He said it was our mum's fault he had to leave, that she hadn't given him enough love. I knew it was a complete lie, but no one else seemed to question it ... or was brave enough to. Your nan never got over losing her husband as well as the respect and love of most of her children."

"Oh, poor Nan," Samantha whispered.

They each allowed quiet tears to fall, looking out at the lake, watching the birds, but adrift in their own individual loss.

Despite Gwen believing her mother was in a beautiful realm of love beyond death, she still found visiting her grave a comfort. There was something about acknowledging the body that lay there, the one that had created and birthed her and was now decomposing back into the earth. It was also a place where sadness was allowed, though sometimes while Gwen was speaking out loud to her mother she laughed, remembering a funny moment they had shared.

The day was closing as she walked back to the car, the last glimpse of sunlight about to drop over Wattledale, beyond the roofs and chimneys in the distance.

"Gwen?"

She shook her head and laughed, unashamed that her eyes revealed recent tears. "Are you stalking me, Russ?"

He smiled tenderly, his own eyes showing their truth of sadness. "Not at all." He looked towards the headstones. "Who are you here visiting?"

"My beautiful mum," Gwen answered. "She died just over a year ago."

"Oh, I'm sorry to hear that, Gwen. I really am."

She nodded. "And you, Russ? Who are you visiting?"

"My wife and daughter. I lost them in the fires a few years ago. While I was out volunteering, my own family was trapped in a ring of fire. They'd never have gotten out, but many days I still wish I hadn't left the house that day and had died with them."

"Oh Russ, that's so sad. Gosh, everyone's got a story, haven't they?"

"Yes, Gwen, they do."

They looked across the cemetery, then back towards each other.

"I don't suppose you'd join me for a meal, Gwen? Life has crossed our paths yet again."

"It has indeed, but not this time, thanks, Russ. I just want to spend some time with Mum in my heart. I think a couple of quiet hours are all I can handle."

He understood and in the last light, they exchanged phone numbers with a mention of lunch sometime. She watched him walk away, his floppy hair bouncing in rhythm with his easy gait.

The clinic looked lonely as she drove down the avenue. Feeling its call, Gwen parked and opened the heavy downstairs door. She stepped into the silence of night in the old building and clicked the hallway light on the left, then climbed the familiar stairs. Soft light from the street outside shone into her darkened room. She lit the jasmine-scented candle. There was no need for anything brighter. Nestled into the purple chair, she stared at the flame, dancing, teasing, insisting it was all that was worth looking at. Despite this, she looked up to see if the spider was weaving its web on the chandelier, the same spider whose web was wiped away by the cleaner each morning.

She squinted until she found it. Despite life giving it plenty of challenges, the spider just turned up and kept going, night after night, rebuilding its life all over. Gwen blew out the candle and allowed the street light to be enough. *Rebuilding life all over*, she thought. It no longer felt impossible. Her mother was dead, but it was time to get back to living.

3

RECIPES FOR LOVE

Jasmine was the first scent of spring to linger longer than a tease. Gwen noticed how the shift in seasons lifted the mood not only of her clients but also people walking down the street. There were more stops for a chat between them. For her, too. She even received a pleasant greeting from Mark, one of her older brothers, when they passed one day. It was only a nod and a "Nice day", but at least it wasn't layered with the usual aggression.

The branches of the willow tree were almost full of leaves, sagging and swaying in the sunshine. Dandelions surrounded it. Out of habit, Gwen picked one. She paused, not knowing what to wish for. Her mother would never join her at this tree again, so there was no point wishing for that. A dandelion might feel magical, but it couldn't raise the dead. She wished instead for a growing relationship with her niece, Samantha.

They had spent time together a few times recently, after Samantha's admission that she wanted to get to know her aunt more. Feeling that relationship bloom while learning to let go of her mother offered a balm to Gwen's heart, a bit of hope to balance the loss. It also helped Gwen to not feel so isolated in a family too fixed in its ways to change or grow. It was exhausting being the odd one out.

She reflected on how easy it had been living away during her backpacking years and wondered if she would ever move again. She felt such freedom when there was no risk of running into family. She had returned to stay close to her mother, but now that she was gone ... the reality struck Gwen again. A part of her still lived in shock that this was her life now, without her mother to share it with.

But there was nowhere else that called. Plus she enjoyed the easy, country pace of Wattledale. It wasn't too small or too big, and she loved her clinic. Avoiding family wasn't a good enough reason to start all over. All she could hope for was a sense of belonging, at least, with someone related. She blew a second dandelion to strengthen her wish for the friendship with her niece to continue blooming. It was a windy day. All the better, thought Gwen, it will give this wish some power. She watched the seed heads fly up and away.

"You hear the words 'passive-aggressive' batted around a lot these days," her client Samira said, stretching out her short, strong legs. Her black hair hung long and straight against her back and a bright yellow pashmina sat comfortably over her shoulders. She frowned and her dark brown eyes met Gwen's.

"Lately I've been understanding more what they mean. I

feel like my closest friend here is just that: passive-aggressive. It's not like I know her that well. I'm pretty new to town. We moved here for my husband's work last year. It's just that as I'm getting to know her a bit better, I'm finding myself a little off balance."

The friend had always seemed a little self-centred, according to Samira, but she was also funny, which was what had kept her there. "And let's face it, we all need more laughter," Samira added.

Over time, though, there were little digs; attempts to make her feel guilty for things like going out with other people, or not telling her friend where she had been when she had just been at the dentist.

"It's like she's addicted to drama. Almost as if she can't be happy being happy. If things are going well, she finds something to stir the pot, so to speak, and create a small rift between us. I'd been feeling sorry for her and able to rise above the nonsense – my parents taught me to be kind. I thought, maybe she's lonely and just holding on a bit tight. But lately I'm starting to think that maybe she's just a nasty person. I don't want to be around that anymore."

She frowned, then stood and stretched her body for a moment, almost unconsciously, and sat again.

"No, it can't be healthy for you, Samira," Gwen replied, "especially if she's doing it repeatedly."

"Yes! But I'm not sure how to extract myself when she only lives a few doors down and sees me come and go. Sanjay, my husband, says to just ignore her and get on with my life. But I find myself walking a massive extra block just to avoid going past her house."

She paused to sip some water. "I don't think this is the sort of friendship that will just fade out, Gwen. There has to be a conversation. I hate to think how she'll talk about me around town after that."

"Maybe the only people who'd believe her aren't the sort whose opinion you'd respect anyway, Samira. I wouldn't be too focused on that."

"Good point, thanks. How do I do this conversation? I dread it and feel nervous already. But some of the things she's said and accused me of lately have really confirmed I can't be friends with her, or even associated with her."

"I think the main thing when you talk with her is not to get stuck in the details. Don't give her ammunition to attack you with. Perhaps just tell her that you're grateful for the time you've spent, but you don't think you're really a good fit … anymore. If you say 'anymore', she may feel at least you thought you were once."

"Goodness. It sounds so easy without her in front of me."

"I get you that might feel a bit awful later, but please remember: you're just as worthy of your own love as the people you give it to. You need to be kind to yourself as well as others."

"Wow. Now, there's a concept! I'm as worthy of my own love as the people I give it to." Samira repeated. "I needed to hear that, Gwen. That line will keep me focused. Bless you!"

After more talk, Gwen accepted the handshake Samira offered in farewell. Since she had grown up in Wattledale, Gwen could often guess who her clients were talking about, but always tried to approach their situations from a neutral, non-judgmental and professional perspective. Still, it wouldn't hurt to whisper a prayer for Samira in extracting herself from the toxicity of Gwen's younger sister, Petra.

∼

While the nights were still cool, the spring sunshine increasingly warmed the days. If Gwen was to get a bushwalk or two in before the real heat of summer arrived, it had to be now. On Tuesday afternoon, her regular afternoon off for self-care, she checked the laces on her boots and began the uphill climb. It wasn't really a bushwalk, she thought to herself, feeling the delight of her muscles in use. The track didn't go for endless hours or offer any surprises once you had walked it once or twice. The only surprises could have been snakes on the path, but that was another reason she chose to walk before the summer arrived. The night had been too cool for them, but it wouldn't be long before that changed and a walker would need to watch out for them.

She reached the mountain peak in an hour and a half, about the same time it usually took her. Once she had done it in less, but missed the enjoyment of the birds and flowering native trees in the process. A few times she had taken much longer, but they had been special days with nature offering one surprise after another, like a wonderfully coloured rock with patterns she had never seen before. She had also stopped to listen to the variety of birdsong along the way. Today it was the view from the top she wanted most, and she was grateful for the clear sky when she arrived there. She looked south across a valley of quilted paddocks and crops. It had been worth the exertion. There was always a breeze up there too, which cooled any walker before they began their descent.

Gwen turned in another direction at the top, looking to the bushland, and wondered about the creatures that lived under the canopy of trees. In that direction, the wilderness stretched as far as the eye could see. It was one of her favourite views, unspoilt by the touch of humans. She turned the whole way around, enjoying the full 360-degree view, and then unpacked her lunch at the wooden picnic table. She thought of the purple chair in her clinic, part of which she called the cushion of a thousand sighs, and wondered how many backsides had sat at this table. She was happy to add to the number once more.

Footsteps came from behind her up the hill, accompanied by laughter and chatter. It was a couple she guessed to be in their sixties.

"Oh hello, love," the woman greeted her.

"You've got the right idea," the man said. "Do you mind if we join you? We try to come up here a few times a year so we've got our lunch too."

With a sweep of her arm and a mouth full of cheese sandwich, Gwen indicated that they were welcome to join her. In between bites of food, a conversation unfolded.

They asked about her work and told her about their own. He said he attended to their floral business in person while she managed all the admin and marketing, "From a quiet office out the back where no one interrupts me," she added with a laugh.

They asked if she had a partner. When Gwen said no, with no explanation, they asked why.

"I guess I feel like my life is full, and I don't really yearn for more. I do have an occasional lover, but in terms of a relationship, I'm just not sure I see any benefit in it. No offence," she added.

"None taken," said the man. "Personally, I couldn't stand being on my own, but we have a few friends the same as you, who feel that their lives are full without a relationship. I almost admire them, but I don't want to be them."

Gwen smiled in reply.

"Just don't close your heart permanently," the man said.

"Life can surprise us all, in the best ways. We only met five years ago and look at us, like lovestruck teenagers in our sixties."

"It's lovely to witness," Gwen said. "Congratulations. My heart's not closed – I'm just not looking for anyone. And my heart's a little battered at the moment. I lost my mother just over a year ago. I'm not sure I have anything in reserve to share."

They offered their condolences and the conversation continued a while longer before Gwen felt a yearning for solitude, and started packing up. The couple began packing away their empty lunch container.

"Are you walking down now too?" she asked them.

"No," the woman said. "We'll stay and enjoy the view a bit longer". The briefest exchange between the couple told Gwen they had other plans. She was happy to leave them and guessed they would have been having sex before she was halfway down the mountain. She smiled to herself, reminded of the fun of love. When all she heard all day were complaints about relationships, and all she'd seen in her family were the kinds of relationships she didn't want, it was healthy to be reminded that some people still actually had fun in partnerships.

～

"I'm ... I guess I'm ... bored?" Gwen's new client Nadia spoke very quietly and with great hesitation. "I've stuck around here because ... because I'm scared to leave. And because I don't want to worry my mother." Her forehead creased with anxiety. "She worries about everything."

Nadia looked at the floor. Gwen waited, comfortable in the silence. However, it seemed that this might be the one client who could outwait her.

She spoke gently. "If I were to ask you what the crux of the problem was, what would you say?"

"Well," said Nadia, "here I am, twenty-four years old, and the most fun I have is—" She paused and looked up to meet Gwen's eyes. "The most fun I have is playing tennis once a week with a group of women who are retired. What's worse is that ... they've all led really interesting lives. They keep telling me to go and see the world!"

"Where would you go, if you did?"

"Oh, I don't know." Nadia's eyes were on the floor again. "Maybe London. Maybe somewhere in Europe. But I wouldn't be able to speak the language."

"Anywhere particular in Europe?" Gwen asked.

For the first time, Nadia's face relaxed. "I'd love to see the Alps, so I guess Switzerland or Austria or Italy. Have you travelled?"

Gwen told Nadia she had, and assured her she would get by fine with English and a little of the local language. "You could enrol in a short language course. That might help you face some of those fears."

The idea seemed to register with Nadia, who agreed it could be fun.

"Now," Gwen prompted, "tell me about your mum and why she's so scared for you".

"Well, she's always been nervous, and she hasn't really done anything with her life, except have me and my older brother. He married someone just like her so now he spends his life doing what my dad does – reassuring his wife that whatever it is she's worried about that day isn't as bad as she thinks."

"I imagine that's a heavy load for you to carry, too. That it might add to your own fears."

Nadia sat in thought and nodded.

"Nadia, all of us have things that scare us. Fear's a survival mechanism. But there are also many fears that aren't justified, that we can absorb from those around us. We either let the fear win or we face it and free ourselves from it. And sometimes we don't even free ourselves from it, but we do the things that scare us anyway."

Nadia sighed. "I'm sure you're right. I just can't imagine being free of fears, yet I've imagined travelling so much I sometimes feel I've actually done those trips."

"You *can* do them. In real life. Another thing to consider is that you may be creating regrets if you don't at least give it a go. You're too young for the weight of those."

"But I'm worried about the stress it will cause my mother – that she'll worry even more."

"Nadia, any loving mother would worry a little about their child travelling overseas, even at 24. But that's the mothering instinct. It shouldn't be a smothering one. It may take some courage and preparation, but honestly, this is *your life*. I don't want you to regret the choices you have or haven't made."

"Yeah. Wow. You're right. I'm already regretting all the time I've wasted."

"And it doesn't mean you don't care. You just deserve a life too, you know."

They chatted a little more until the session concluded. Gwen said goodbye at the door and watched Nadia jump the last three stairs on the way out of the building. The young woman turned and waved goodbye, calling back up to her, "Thank you so much, Gwen! Bye!".

Gwen sat down in the purple chair, reflecting on her

own travelling years as a younger woman. She suddenly craved some excitement, a good sign her will to go on was reawakening. Travel didn't feel like the pull, but some excitement needed to be found. Or at the least, some fun.

~

Clapping echoed through the café's leafy courtyard. Gwen bowed, acknowledging the welcome of her friends. Five familiar faces, as well as one she didn't know, smiled and welcomed her to their table.

"Thank you, all," she said, walking up to them, a little surprised at how good it felt to be there. "It's lovely to be back." Hugs came from all she knew.

The stranger introduced herself as Susan and hugged Gwen in greeting. "It's great to finally meet you, Gwen. I joined the group about a year ago." Gwen squeezed her arm warmly, with a quiet hello.

"Sit down! Sit down! It's so good to have you back!" Nicole said, laughing.

All of the women worked for themselves. Gwen had been enjoying a monthly lunch with them for three years, but had pulled back after her mother's breakdown. Following her mother's death, she retreated further. The group had initially come together to support each other in self-employment, but it had grown into something much more. Absorbing their joy on her return, Gwen acknowledged that they were the fun she needed.

It was chaos for a while, with excited, overlapping conversations and lots of laughter. Gwen sat and smiled, feeling loved. Tears welled and she gulped them down. She realised how lonely she had been for people who appreciated her as she was. She had thought her mother was the only one, but in her pain had forgotten the importance of positive friends and connection. She wiped away a couple of rogue tears that escaped.

Nicole, always the most organised and vocal, called for quiet. "We all know Gwen's the listener in this town. And I don't know about the rest of you, but I'd like to honour her with my own listening and hear how she's going. Everyone else feel the same?" They all agreed, some enthusiastically, a couple more gently.

"Gosh. I don't even know where to start, other than I hadn't realised how much I needed to be here with you all. Thank you." Glistening eyes around the table matched Gwen's own. "It's been a hard road, that's for sure. I miss Mum so much. But there comes a time when you have to get back to life, or on with a new one, despite the pain. And that's where I'm trying to be."

She talked about her work and the satisfaction it still brought her, and how the distraction of her client's problems helped her detach from her own, even if just in the moment. She explained how she had felt even more disconnected from her family since her mother died, except for the surprising new relationship with her niece.

She also admitted to her hope of starting to feel a little normal again, even though she didn't really believe in the concept of normal. They laughed at that, knowing that as a psychologist Gwen had a broad acceptance of humanity. People who might not be considered normal by the general population were still normal to her. So there was a lot of freedom in her wanting to feel a little normal again. It could mean anything that made her happy.

Nicole asked if there was a man in her life. Gwen looked

a little startled, never having been asked that before in the group.

"No," she said. "I'm still the independent, cat-loving woman you knew before."

"Just checking," Nicole said, and laughed.

"Mind you, I did happen to have a rather pleasant afternoon recently in the back of a campervan with a man whose voice was like melted chocolate."

Squeals and shouts of glee bounced off the leafy courtyard's brick walls, making other diners look up and smile at whatever the excitement was. It was enough of an answer to get them off her case. Russ suddenly came to mind. Gwen shook her head clear of the thought. "Anyway, let's hear about you lot!"

It seemed that life wanted Gwen and Russ to become friends, having placed them unexpectedly in front of each other three times now. The first time, Gwen had just been struck in the head by a teenage boy's skateboard and Russ had helped her up. The next was them unexpectedly meeting up at the same coastal resort, a fairly long drive from their area. They had watched whales pass by while they sat on the headland and chatted. Recently, they had learned more about each other in one minute than in the other two occasions combined, when their timing found them both raw and open at the cemetery. Since then, there had been two phone chats – not long or deep, but enjoyable.

Another Tuesday afternoon had rolled around. Gwen had accepted a lunch invitation from Russ. With no expectations or even any anticipation, she drove to meet him. He was easy company and, given the heaviness of the last year, that in itself was a blessing. Following his suggestion of a particular village pub, she drove up the small hill and parked, adjusted her light jacket and headed inside. The days were warming up with spring sunshine, but evenings still cooled the old buildings down. She was happy to see a wood fire burning.

"Gwen!" Russ called from a nearby table. She smiled and joined him.

"Hi, Russ," she said, taking off her jacket. "I think you've got us the best table in the place. Did you book it?"

"Yes! The view is wonderful. I came here with my dad recently and I decided then that this was the only table I ever wanted to eat at."

Grateful for his foresight, she looked out across the rural valley dotted with an occasional farmhouse, and to the huge sky above it. "I've never been here. I can't believe that now, to be honest. I'm just not much of a drinker so I don't tend to hang out in pubs. But this is truly perfect." She turned back from the window and smiled across at him. "I hope the food lives up to the setting."

"It will. Don't worry." His confidence left her peaceful. She was famished, having skipped snacks in order to enjoy lunch fully.

Their talk had gone to a new level since the brief encounter at the cemetery. They knew each other's deepest pain already. Small talk would have seemed out of place. Now it was only a matter of filling in the gaps that led to Gwen's loss of her mother and Russ's loss of his wife and daughter. It didn't feel as painful to share with someone who already understood such levels of loss.

Lunch arrived and confirmed Russ's opinion of the food.

She had ordered smoked trout and seasoned vegetables. The balance of herbs smelled perfect. She couldn't eat until she had satisfied the urge to close her eyes and inhale the scents that danced under her nostrils. Opening her eyes, she found Russ watching her intently.

"Glad you like it," he said quietly.

Gwen smiled and took her first bite. "Mmm, this is so good!"

She felt like they had been friends for ages and told him so. He agreed that their connection was an easy one. When the waiter came to tell them that the room had to close since lunch hours were over, they realised they had been talking for three hours. With full bellies and nurtured hearts, they walked outside. The breeze carried a chill. Russ offered to help Gwen with her jacket.

"No, it's OK. The car's warm, so it's best I get in it! Thanks for a lovely afternoon, Russ. Drive safely."

She accepted the hug he offered, then quickly got into her car, turned the motor on, and waved as she drove out towards the road. Glancing in the rear-view mirror, she saw him still standing there watching her, the chilly breeze blowing his curls wild.

Gwen opened the door to see Samantha holding up a rolling pin with a smile. "I hope this is good?" Her niece had never been in Gwen's home before.

"Perfect. Come on in."

Through a recent conversation, they had discovered that

her mother's lemon meringue pie was one of their favourite dishes.

"I hope we do Nan justice!" Samantha laughed. "Although I think we need to accept we likely won't."

"Well, we're doing her justice simply by celebrating her memory this way."

"I can't believe she still made her own pastry from scratch."

"Yes, and now we'll try it too!" Gwen laughed.

They read the recipe together, brushed the flour off their hands onto the pretty aprons Samantha had brought for the occasion, checked each other's measurements, and concentrated as if their lives depended on it. Samantha said it was serious business trying to do her grandmother justice.

With the pie in the oven, they sat in the patch of sunshine in Gwen's courtyard. Claudia, usually unsociable with visitors, jumped onto Samantha's lap and fell asleep. After many questions about Samantha's life, Samantha started questioning Gwen, including whether there were any men friends in her life.

"I keep being asked that lately. No one asks me for years, and now here I am being asked it again!"

"Well?"

"No, I'm not interested in a relationship. But as far as friends go, I do have a new one in a guy called Russ. He seems like a good guy," Gwen said.

"And you don't fancy him at all?"

"No. He's not the kind of guy I usually go for."

"Hmm," Samantha murmured.

"What's that supposed to mean?"

"Well, how did it go with the kinds of men you're usually attracted to? I mean, you've been single for a long time now."

"Single by choice," Gwen insisted.

"I'm just saying that maybe you should give this guy a go, because maybe you've been going for the wrong kinds of men until now. Otherwise, you'd still be with one of them."

A sweet fragrance of lemon and pastry wafted into the courtyard.

Gwen jumped up. "Saved by the pie!"

Her niece put Claudia gently on the ground and followed Gwen into the kitchen, but she didn't give up on the subject easily. Gwen let her know that Russ was only interested in her as a friend, so any theories Samantha might be offering were entirely hypothetical.

"Well, Auntie Gwen, maybe you could at least open your heart a little and see him as a man instead of a mate. I can guarantee he's already noticed that you're a woman! Just see what happens."

"Oh shoosh, will you?" Gwen laughed. "Get the plates down from over there. This pie smells divine."

She realised her niece had a point, and for the first time in longer than she cared to admit she quietly allowed her heart to open, just a little.

The Wattledale farmers' market was on every second weekend. Gwen liked to get there early, particularly with the days getting warmer. Spring was certainly upon them. She hated to think of vegetables, fresh from the ground, left to wilt in the heat while waiting for a buyer. The placement of some of the stalls meant that some of them copped the full sun by 7 am.

It was a glorious morning, with lots of early risers stocking up. The grass was dewy as she chose her fresh produce. She was especially excited to see the beets. They had been extra sweet lately and she loved to add them to other things for her juice.

One of her ex-schoolmates was setting up his keyboard and microphone. He had left school as an uncool, unnoticed student and returned to the area as a hunky musician. He had been the talk of the town when he had first arrived back. He was friendly to anyone who said hello, but was more interested in his music than people. Gwen didn't mind. She had no desire to force a conversation, and she loved his tunes. She put her vegetables into the padded cooler bags in her shaded car, placed a few ice bricks strategically around them, and then joined the queue for the coffee van.

With her hot chocolate and a freshly baked croissant in hand, she found a spot near the music and relaxed. Her old schoolmate certainly knew how to cover popular songs. His guitar case was soon filled with coins and the occasional note. Gwen had asked him once, when she'd spotted him at the craft market in Pebbly Creek, if he had any original songs. He had told her he had plenty, but they didn't open people's wallets. When people recognised a song, it triggered good feelings and they dropped money in his guitar case. It had been quite a long conversation, given his reputation for silence.

Gwen was happy to listen to anything. His repertoire was vast and she found herself delighted in being reminded of songs she had forgotten.

"Well, well, well, if it's not the high and mighty Gwen."

She didn't need to look up to know it was her younger sister. "Oh, hi Petra. Pull up a seat if you like."

Her sister did. Gwen waited for another line of attack, but the music distracted her sister right away.

"Wow," Petra said when the song finished. "Wow. I could almost cry, that was so good."

"Absolutely. Do you remember him from school? He was in my class."

"Sort of," Petra said. "Gwen ... there's something I need to ask you."

"Oh. OK. Sure. What's up?"

"Oh, God. I don't even know how to ask."

Her sister bit her bottom lip and frowned in concentration. Gwen waited and enjoyed the cool breeze for a moment until Petra continued.

"Um ... I've been thinking of coming to see you at your clinic. I think I might have some problems."

"Petra, I couldn't see you as a client – you're my sister – but we can talk as sisters. You can talk to me anytime. What's going on?"

"I feel I should pay you for your time, Gwen. It's not like I've ever been particularly nice to you, or like you owe me anything."

"Well, why don't you tell me a bit about it now, since we're here anyway?"

Petra explained that she had recently lost a new friend, a woman called Samira whose company she really enjoyed. "I was so mean to her. I knew it at the time. I didn't want to push her away, but I really enjoyed seeing how far I could go. But the thing is, I do it to anyone I care about. It's like I have to reject them before they get to know me, and realise I'm nothing special and then reject me."

Gwen's heart stirred for her sister, who had described the pattern perfectly. It was one she had witnessed in Petra for years.

"Well, that's a pretty wise observation of yourself, but I'm not sure it's what you *always* do."

"I do it often enough, Gwen, believe me."

"I'm sorry you feel like you have to. Everyone has a good person in there somewhere and that includes you, Petra. Do you have any close friends these days, besides Samira?"

"I have some friendly acquaintances, I guess. We play volleyball and then have a few drinks later. We've been doing that for a couple of years. But no, no one really close. As soon as I start feeling close to a friend, I sabotage it and turn into Madam Awful. Anyway, that's enough to dump on you on a sunny morning at the market."

"Let's catch up another time then."

"Thanks, Gwen, but you do know that if we talk about this stuff, I'll probably attack you sometime too."

"Oh, I'm used to it," Gwen joked gently. "I can handle you. But I also know how hard it's been losing Mum and how it's sent us all into a bit of a spin. Anyway, if you push me too far, I may just push you back a little."

Petra smiled and then hugged her tightly, something she had never done. Gwen received the hug, holding her younger sister until she let go in her own time. Afterwards, when Gwen sat alone reflecting, she sent some love to her mother, who would have been pleased to witness what had unfolded. While Gwen felt too guarded to take huge pleasure in it, she did feel hope.

❧

"My wife sent me here as an ultimatum," Marco explained as he walked into the clinic.

"Hi, Marco. Nice to meet you," Gwen replied, gesturing to the purple chair. "Please, sit down."

"Hi. Yes, sorry. Anyway, she thinks I'm a workaholic. Actually, I *am* a workaholic. Hell, I feel like I'm at an AA meeting. 'Hello. My name is Marco and I'm an alcoholic.' It's not the same thing. I just like working hard, but if I don't slow down, she says I'll lose her and the kids. My doctor also said I have to slow down or I'll drop dead. But he's overexaggerating."

"Is he?" Gwen asked. "You know, Marco, you're making fun of AA but it does amazing things for people. Workaholism is an addiction too, and any addiction has the potential to heal through connection with others. Are you spending much quality time with your family?"

"No, not really. Not enough for them, anyway. And perhaps not enough for me. My children are growing up quickly. I looked at my daughter Francesca the other day and felt like she'd jumped two years since I'd last looked at her properly."

As they spoke, Gwen admired his ability to receive her direct questions without offence, answering honestly, if somewhat matter-of-factly. By the end of the session, Marco had realised that he was using work to mask some long-term marital problems. He didn't want to lose his wife, but felt he wasn't the whole problem in the marriage.

Gwen understood that in situations like this, the problem might not lie with just one person. Both likely had expectations and needs that the other wasn't meeting – or possibly didn't even know about. She recommended a couples therapist she knew.

She had taken to sitting in the purple chair after almost every client, to reflect on what they had shared. Its high back and raised arms were comforting; it was like being cocooned in softness and protection. It was a bonus that she hadn't considered when she had first fallen in love with the chair and bought it on the spot. It also explained why most of her clients relaxed so easily in it.

Providing them with a space to talk things out allowed them to untangle their thoughts and sometimes find their own answers. She loved all she learned about life through her role, helping to steer clients to possible solutions. It was certainly an ever-deepening practice of compassion, too. Some of the stories she heard ripped her heart out. Yet the level of resilience she often witnessed inspired her at the same time. Some of the conversations were also fascinating. It sometimes still amazed her, after years of clinical practice, just where a conversation could end up, considering where it had begun.

She pushed herself up from the purple chair and tidied her desk. With all the files locked away and the plants watered, she closed the door for another day. Riding her bike home most days was a great antidote for her work. The breeze often blew the day away completely before she reached her front door to be welcomed by Claudia, the cat.

One of the things Gwen found hardest about her mother's death was remembering. Something would happen and she would think she must tell her mother when she next saw her, or would imagine the phone conversation they would have, the laughter or the understanding shared. Then she would remember. There were no more phone conversations to be had, ever. No hugs. No smell of her mother's favourite perfume on her skin. Nothing but memories that were often too painful to sit with for long.

Besides the cookbooks and a couple of other small things she had taken from her mother's place before her siblings arrived like a pack of scavengers, she also had a shirt her mother had worn often. Gwen had taken it from the washing basket in the care home that her mother had been living in. It still carried her mother's scent. She slept with it for months, inhaling it deeply, crying into it, holding it tightly.

One morning she realised it no longer smelled of her mother, but of her own house. She leaned against the chair in her bedroom for support and sobbed. Her hands almost reached out for something invisible, anything to stop the scent from slipping away forever. But it was already gone, and there was nothing left that smelled of her mother. Time had erased her scent from the planet.

Gwen slid to the floor and curled into a ball, clutching the shirt to her. No tightness of curling was enough to ease the grief.

In the many months since her mother had died, more than a year ago, she hadn't washed the shirt. Instead, she had hung it in the sunshine and let that wash it. Now, although she couldn't smell her mother on it, her touch was still there somewhere, somehow.

She fell asleep on the lounge for a few hours and woke in the mid-afternoon. With her latest bout of grief released, her spirit was weary but a little lighter. She decided to cook something from her mother's recipes. When the sweet scent of chocolate cherry slice filled her kitchen, Gwen laughed out loud. Her mother's scent was not gone. It lived on through every meal her daughter cooked from the same recipes. The tuna mornay had brought her dear mum back into the present, memories bursting alive at the smell. The lemon meringue pie that she and Samantha had cooked strengthened family bonds as it had done when her mother cooked it. With the chocolate cherry slice, her mother stood beside her, guiding her, commending her efforts, and sharing the moment. If Gwen couldn't keep her mother's scent alive in her shirt, she could do so through her cooking.

She cut the slice, admiring its perfect consistency, and decided that from this day onward she would use her special antique plates whenever she was honouring her mother through cooking. She placed a piece of the slice on a plate. It sat within the circle of delicate blue flowers painted around the rim.

She carried it to her little table in the courtyard. The small peach tree growing in a large pot in the corner was in full bloom, complete with sparrows chattering away on its branches. Inhaling the sweetness of the slice, she raised it to the sunshine.

"Here's to you, Mum."

As Gwen savoured the first bite slowly, the cherries, dark chocolate and coconut melded in a rich symphony of flavour. Her heart was nurtured, dipped in memories.

"Here's to you, Mum," she repeated, this time in a loving whisper.

She took another bite and smiled.

4

WHISPERS FROM THE WILLOW TREE

Gwen was aware she was wasting too much time on Instagram, but it was sometimes the relaxing distraction she needed – and not all of her scrolling was pointless. There was a guy she followed called Dr David Hamilton. He was a scientist who translated complicated things into everyday language. Gwen found his videos fascinating. In one, he spoke of time speeding up for adults because they do the same things too often, whereas time felt like forever for children because they embrace new things regularly. Gwen decided to make an effort to introduce more variety into her life.

Having regular clients sitting in the purple chair depending on her ear and counsel, and having Claudia, the cat, at home insisting on being fed at the exact same time every day meant there were certain routines that needed to be honoured. She didn't resist them, but had other routines designed to support herself. These included riding her bicycle to and from work most days, meeting her business friends for lunch once a month, eating lunch out of the clinic as often as possible, and taking Tuesday afternoons off work.

At least on her Tuesday afternoons she could honour her commitment to as much variety as possible. The previous week she had watched a movie at home in her pyjamas, rather than put herself under pressure to drive somewhere – something she often did for fun. She had bought a slice of strawberry cheesecake on the way home from her morning at the clinic, greeted Claudia, made a huge cup of coffee, and stayed glued to her large, comfortable sofa and the remote control all afternoon. Spring was transitioning into summer, but she had been gifted a cool day. After adjusting the extra cushions, Gwen snuggled into the afternoon. She grabbed the colourful knitted blanket she had picked up at a charity shop years before for $2 and threw it over her legs, burying Claudia underneath. Sometimes she just needed some nurturing and if it always had to come from herself since her mother died, then so be it.

~

Hesitation was Gwen's natural reaction when a sibling's name showed up on her ringing phone. Tonight was no exception.

"Hi, Jackie," she answered her older sister.

"Oh, you're not going to believe this one!" There was rarely a 'Hello' with Jackie, and certainly never a 'How are you?'.

Gwen could almost have called the shift in family dynamics since her mother died *interesting* if it wasn't so exhausting. Her siblings seemed panicked, almost manic, as they tried to find their new way forward.

"What's up, Jackie? I don't have much time." *I don't have much energy, more like.*

"What? What sort of welcome is that?"

"What do you want, Jackie?" Gwen asked.

"Well, I think Harold's having an affair. He keeps coming home late. Never asks for sex, which would be a relief if I wasn't so suspicious."

"And you've asked him?"

"Of course, I've asked him!" she shrieked. Gwen moved the phone away from her ear and switched it to speaker mode. Claudia looked up from the sofa unimpressed. "Of course, he denies it. Says he's been playing squash with his workmates and wants to save his energy for that. The lying sod even puts sweaty sports clothes in the washing basket to cover his tracks."

"Uh," Gwen hesitated. "Maybe he's actually telling the truth."

"Oh, that's so typical of you, Gwen."

"What is?"

"Taking Harold's side against me."

"Jackie," Gwen replied, "I'm tired of being criticised by you, and I'm tired of being a dumping ground for your problems. You don't know me at all, and you don't even try to. So I'm going to say goodbye now." She hung up, not waiting to hear her sister's reaction, counted to three and ignored the call back.

Her heart was beating hard. It was scary to stand up for herself instead of choosing silence or avoidance. There was freedom in it too, though, and a quiet smile crept onto her face. Claudia jumped off the sofa and rubbed against Gwen's leg for attention. She picked the cat up and stroked her.

Gwen's eyes blurred into a stare while her mind took it in: she no longer felt obliged to keep the peace with her siblings for her mother's sake.

Who knew that being an orphan could actually be freeing? *Well, I'm not an orphan*, she reminded herself. As far as she knew, her father was still alive on the planet somewhere with his next-generation family and new wife. He was dead to her, though. It had been liberating to realise she wasn't obliged to him, or even connected to him, anymore. If Gwen had ever had any respect for him, it was long gone after he had dumped them all and left her mother with almost nothing except seven kids. She would feel the same if he was dead. Dying wouldn't make him a saint.

She walked into the courtyard and looked up, trying to find a star or two in the cloudy night. Claudia purred and accepted her mindless stroking.

It was a gentle ride to work, with the breeze in her favour. Gwen locked her bike to the rack outside the hobby shop and headed to her favourite coffee vendor. Shortly after, she climbed the familiar stairs holding the hot cup, automatically stepping with just the right amount of pressure so that step number six didn't squeak.

Her phone pinged with a text on the way up. Once inside her clinic room, she sat in the purple chair, bought for her clients to sit in but increasingly being where she sat, and opened her phone.

Dinner tonight? it read.

Dinner felt like so much more than lunch. She put the

phone away in the top drawer of her desk. Ten seconds later, she pulled it back out and replied, *Sure*.

Russ was easy company and if it meant she was genuinely busy if any family members phoned, it was worth it. Plus it was only dinner.

~

It was all new clients today. Gwen had modified her methods from those she had learned at university, giving her more freedom in how she conducted her sessions. This meant she no longer officially practised as a psychologist or counsellor, as she was qualified to, so her clients were unable to claim her sessions through their healthcare funds. She also lost certain rebates from the government by choosing this path, but calling herself a 'Listener' felt more comfortable.

Doing things her own way hadn't affected her business or her reputation. The waiting list for a session with Gwen's ear was a minimum of six weeks.

She followed the coffee with a glass of water and read the completed form sent in by her next client. Then it was time to welcome him to the purple chair. Ricky settled into it and placed his reading glasses and book on the table beside him.

"I feel a bit ridiculous being here and paying to talk to someone," he said.

Gwen smiled. "Don't worry, you're not the first person to say that."

His black, curly hair was blending into grey. The depths of his dark brown eyes revealed sadness and confusion as he continued. "I mean, what state is the world in when we have to pay for a stranger to listen to us?" He rolled up the sleeves of his checked shirt. Fine dust from his work boots settled on the floor.

"Sometimes, Ricky, people find it much easier to speak with a stranger than their own kin."

"You're not wrong there, actually. My mob can't listen to save their lives. OK. So this is what I need to talk about. I've got nine kids, all grown and gone. But there's one daughter who I just can't stand. I get angry as soon as I look at her. Always have. My wife said if I don't do something about it, she's going to make my life hell. I couldn't live without the missus, so here I am."

"Do you love this daughter, even if you can't stand her?"

"Oh, I guess so. I mean, she's my blood and I don't wish harm on her. I'm not that much of a monster."

"Did you feel loved by your own parents?"

A flash of sadness crossed Ricky's eyes. "No, not really. In fact, I don't think my mother could stand me. Oh!" He shook his head.

"Can you describe how that felt?"

"Like I wasn't wanted and it was the worst feeling in the world, wanting someone to love you so much, but realising you're just a thorn in their side and they can't stand you. I spent my whole childhood wondering what I did wrong and trying to find ways to fix it. None of them worked."

"I'm so sorry to hear that." She waited a moment and then asked, "Have you noticed you used the same term to describe your daughter – that you can't stand her?"

"Oh no." His anguished gaze turned to the floor before looking back to Gwen. "That poor girl. How can I not stand one of my own children?"

"Is she like you in any way, besides having a parent who can't stand her?"

Ricky was silent for a long time. At one point he glanced at her, seeming unsure of whether to fill the quietness. Gwen waved her hand slightly, permitting the extension of silence for as long as needed.

When he did look at her again, his voice quivered. "Yeah, she is."

Gwen simply nodded. After another minute of silence, Ricky looked around the room and then back to her.

"She's so much like me it isn't funny, Gwen. She's the black sheep, and so was I, the one who was just a bit different and copped it as a result. She was a good kid and is a great woman. I'm a little jealous of her at times, to be honest. She's really good at what she does, and she's strong. Maybe that's why I keep trying to knock her down."

He frowned then shook his head.

"How the hell do I fix this? I've been such a prick."

"Well. An apology from a parent can go a long way. It'd be a start at least." Ricky nodded, acknowledging this, and Gwen continued, "You also have to forgive yourself, Ricky. We need to look into your own pain, because if it wasn't still eating at you, you wouldn't be treating your daughter the way you have been. Let's consider some ways to be kinder to yourself, to start that process of healing."

Not long before Ricky's session, Gwen had received a text from the client following Ricky, saying they weren't feeling well and wouldn't be coming in. Sometimes she filled those newly vacant spaces with people on her waitlist. Sometimes, as today, she didn't, and was grateful to have extended time for Ricky. With her guidance he wrote a list of things hurting him, things he could do that were kinder to himself, and what he would say to his daughter once he had the courage. His sniffles rang through the room as he wrote. A few tears landed on the paper.

~

Why does dinner have such different connotations to lunch? Gwen asked herself. She and Russ had already shared a few happy occasions in the middle of the day. But they had been safe and restricted, with a time limit and an afternoon to escape into afterwards. She wasn't looking for more than that. Her relationship history was hardly encouraging. When she added to that the relationship between her parents that she'd witnessed growing up, it was not easy to feel optimistic.

Gwen's main resistance was she loved her freedom. She liked not having to tell someone what time she would be home. Sometimes they were small things that others might not think of as freedom, like burping as loud as she could after a great meal at home and laughing at herself, hitting the road spontaneously on a weekend with an unknown destination, or going to bed as early as she needed without needing to justify it to anyone. In her experience and observations, most relationships, even the good ones, extinguished spontaneity in a very short time.

She stopped herself. They were all assumptions and excuses. Of course she could still go to bed early if she wanted to, *and* the rest. She reminded herself that it was only dinner. Russ wasn't asking her to move in with him. Despite her early resistance even to their friendship, she couldn't deny she always felt better after time in his company. That was worth noting, she told herself as she stood in front of her wardrobe, confused by choice.

She decided on her flared burnt orange pants, matched with a black halter top, purple and orange earrings and her favourite forest green shoes. After dabbing her earthy essential oil blend on her neck and wrists, she was in her car and on the way.

The road between Wattledale and Kestrel usually took just over a dozen songs. There was only one route, but other than needing to watch out for the occasional kangaroo, it was a straight and easy drive. She saw the flashing lights from a distance and sighed, slowing down as she drove closer. Cars were turning around. Gwen pulled up near the temporary traffic light. She turned off the music as a man in a high-visibility vest walked over to her window. She wound it down.

"There's been a gas leak, love. The road'll be closed all night, sorry. It should be fine tomorrow, but we can't let anyone through in the dark as there are things we can't be fully sure of until morning."

Gwen thanked him and rested her head back, blew out, took another deep breath, blew out again, and manoeuvred her car to head back to Wattledale. Russ handled it well when she called from the vehicle, saying he would call soon to arrange a new date.

Date: she couldn't wrap her head around the word, though he had used it in the literal sense, not the romantic one.

~

The last thing Gwen felt like doing was going home to the cat and having to cook dinner for herself. This was the kind of situation where, before her mother's breakdown, she would have phoned her mother and dropped in at her place, or taken her out to dinner. She phoned her niece Samantha instead.

"Hey. I don't suppose you're free to go out for dinner? My plans fell through due to some gas leak out on Farmer Road. I can't get through."

"Oh, Auntie Gwen, another night for sure, but I can't tonight. I'm with some friends already."

"No worries, sweetheart. But let's do it sometime anyway. It'd be fun."

Fun, she thought as she hung up. Restlessness ate at her. If she had been a drinker, she might have bought a bottle of wine and gone home to write herself off. Since it only took one glass to do that and she had to work the next morning, she scrapped that idea. She was all dressed up with nowhere to go and pondered what to do. Since it was Thursday, a midweek night, she wrote off the idea of phoning anyone from her business girls' group. Most were working mothers.

Driving past the shops and pubs in her town, she had no idea what she was looking for. She finally decided on a meal for one in one of Wattledale's restaurants and parked the car. She strolled along, considering which one she might choose, browsing in shop windows, grateful for her resistance to dressing up too much for Russ. Her comfortable shoes made the evening stroll more enjoyable than high heels would have.

"Excuse me?"

Gwen turned to see a man about her age with a trimmed beard and a warm smile.

"Yes?"

"I've just arrived in town. I'm here for the night, then back on the road tomorrow. Are you local? And if so, can you recommend somewhere good to eat, please?"

"Yes, I'm local. It depends on what you like. The Thai's pretty good but I'm biased, due to an addiction to ginger." The man chuckled. "Also, the pub up the hill there has good meals." His eyes followed her pointed finger. "So does the bowling club, if you don't mind being surrounded by old men still wearing their white bowling outfits and so drunk that they should have gone home hours ago."

"I think ginger works for me. Point me in the direction of the Thai restaurant, please. Or, better still, would you care to join me? I've been on the road for 11 hours today, listening to podcasts and old music. A two-way conversation may save my sanity."

"Mine, too," Gwen laughed. "Sure." She extended her hand. "I'm Gwen."

He shook her hand. "Declan. Nice to meet you, Gwen." They walked the short distance to the restaurant and the smell of ginger welcomed them inside.

It was a long time since she had slept beside anyone, so it didn't surprise her that she was wakeful, lying next to Declan. The long day on the road had caught up with him, and he slept deeply beside her. The fluorescent light from the carpark shone into the bathroom of his motel room, allowing some to filter into the room itself.

Gwen had never been one to sneak off from a lover, having had that done to her once as a young woman. It had left her feeling used and awful. Eyeing the pen and paper next to the bed encouraged her, though. She could at least leave him a note. She had work tomorrow and didn't want to spend the night looking at the ceiling when she had a comfortable bed waiting at home. She rose softly and dressed, then took the pen and paper to the bathroom, closed the door and wrote.

It was a pleasure to spend time with you, Declan. I had to go home due to an early start tomorrow. I hope the rest of your trip is a great one. Gwen. x

She turned off the light, allowing the light filtering in from outside to lead the way back to the bed. She hesitated before smiling, recalling how, in the movies, the note was often left on the pillow of the absent party. She placed it on her pillow, picked up her small handbag, tiptoed to the door and pulled it softly closed behind her.

They had been a good match, physically, she decided on the short drive home. The sex had been great for two people who didn't know each other's bodies. Her own felt satisfied, but she was also aware of a vacant space within her, an abyss of emptiness. She had known it a few times in her life, often enough to recognise the trigger: sex without love. She set herself a mental reminder to recall this feeling next time she was tempted to take on another unknown lover. The price to pay was becoming more than the gift received, as tempting as it could be.

She fell asleep in her own comfortable bed. As well as the emptiness gnawing at Gwen, a feeling of betrayal accompanied her into dreaming. She didn't owe Russ anything, she justified to herself. They weren't a couple. But her sleep was a troubled one.

~

Gwen liked Margo immediately. Large red clay beads, with colourful designs painted on them, bounced off Margo's hot pink top. These were balanced by a flowing red skirt and the outfit completed with a comfortable-looking pair of hot pink shoes. It wasn't an outfit put together by chance.

"Welcome, Margo. It's lovely to meet you," Gwen said as she shook her hand, offered her a cup of mint tea which Margo accepted, and pointed her to the purple chair. Once seated, Margo had a brief look around, took a breath and jumped straight in.

"I realised a long time ago that I just don't actually like people. And while I'm at peace with that, I'm getting tired of other people acting like there's something wrong with me. Really, I wish people would just leave me alone, but they seem to want to fix me."

Gwen nodded in understanding.

"I'm not trying to fix *them*," said Margo, "though, goodness me, some of them certainly need some fixing!" She laughed loudly. It was not something Gwen saw often in her clinic or life: someone laughing with such presence and lack of inhibition.

"So why are you actually here then, Margo? You're clearly at peace with yourself and the choices you're making."

"Yes, I am. I really love being on my acreage, with the creek bubbling by and the wildlife about. I'm not saying I'm perfect – I'm sure if we dug deep enough, we'd find something there to be thrashed out. But generally, I'm pretty happy with my life. But the reason I'm here – well, it may put you in a bit of a compromising position, I'm afraid."

"Oh. I see. Tell me then."

"It's just that one of my neighbours is coming to see you next week and I was kind of hoping you might be able to drop a line or two in about allowing people to live their own lives the way they choose."

"Oh," Gwen said. "Yes. That is a tricky situation. Oh, dear!"

They both chuckled before Margo spoke again.

"I know people think we all have this primal need to mate, but I don't think it applies to everybody. I've had relationships – one even lasted a couple of decades – but I'm just happier on my own. I'm also at a time in life when I choose ease over anything else. I come to town for supplies, but even this little town's getting too busy for me. Some of us are just naturally reclusive, and it's not because we're all traumatised and avoiding being hurt. We're just genuinely happier on our own."

The conversation flowed on for a while longer before Gwen explained that she couldn't honour Margo's request. It was a conflict of interest and, professionally speaking, she needed to maintain strict boundaries between her work with different clients. She suggested that Margo write a note to her neighbour, but she declined.

"It's OK, thanks, Gwen. Just being heard today has helped. That's a good start, and I understand your position. I just had to try!" She laughed loudly.

Gwen found herself quietly smiling after the door downstairs had closed behind Margo. The woman certainly had some cheek to have asked, but the peace that Margo emanated was real. Gwen didn't witness that in many of her clients, or in many people she came across anywhere. She certainly hadn't witnessed it in herself for a very long time.

∾

Samantha's 21st birthday was fast approaching. This was different to her nephew's 21st. She couldn't rush off to the coast to avoid it, as she had with his. She and Samantha were enjoying an ever-strengthening relationship. She had to be there. She wanted to be. She just didn't want to be around the rest of the family, who would also be there.

Gwen thought of Margo, at peace on her own, accepting that she was happier that way. But even with her reclusive lifestyle, her client couldn't avoid other people. As much as Gwen sometimes hated to admit it to herself, her family were her best teachers. They helped her to develop compassion – sometimes for herself, sometimes for them – but most of all, they taught her how to grow the inner strength to stay grounded in who she was regardless of how they saw her.

On the night of the 21st, she strapped the light onto her bike and cycled to the home of one of her older brothers, Mark, Samantha's father. The noise from the backyard in the dusk light indicated a large consumption of alcohol already. The screeching voice of one of her sisters was a pitch above the general tones. Samantha clearly didn't have control of the music. Her brother's favourite punk music from the 1980s could be heard on the street.

"Auntie Gwen!" her niece called. "Hi!"

Perhaps the birthday girl was already too drunk to remember that she didn't want their association known to the family. Well, they soon would, Gwen thought. Samantha threw her arms around Gwen and led her over to her friends.

"Everyone! This is my Auntie Gwen and she's the coolest member of this family! We're also a fabulous cooking team, aren't we, Auntie Gwen?"

"We are indeed, my dear niece. We are indeed."

Gwen linked her arm through Samantha's and steered her away for a moment.

"Are you crazy or drunk?" she asked Samantha. "I thought you wanted to keep our friendship quiet."

Samantha laughed. "I'm neither. I've just learnt from you how much freedom there is in being yourself."

"Yes, but sweetheart, it took a lot of pain and work to get there."

"Well," Samantha sighed, "that begins today for me. It's my birthday, so I may just get away with it!"

"Gwen?" They turned to see her younger sister Petra standing there.

"Hi, Petra. Nice to see you," Gwen said. It was only recently that Petra had run into Gwen at a local farmer's market and spoken about her unhappiness and her desire to be a better person. It was a baby step in the healing of their relationship, but a step, nonetheless.

"Uh, you too." Petra looked uncertainly at Samantha. "Are you two friends or something?"

Samantha admitted they were, kissed Gwen on the cheek and returned to her friends. Gwen steered Petra to a couple of chairs under the swaying party lights linked from one tree in the backyard to another. They chatted lightly at first, Petra looking around to see who was watching them. The conversation soon deepened as Gwen listened to her little sister with compassion. Petra's healing was painful, as she tried to break unhealthy patterns of self-sabotage in friendships.

Gwen understood from her own life and from her clients that most healing brought with it some form of pain. It usually had quite a depth to surface from. As long as the pull forward was strong and the vision of hope was clear enough, any pain could be surmountable. It just took time, a lot of mindfulness, and especially self-kindness.

For as long as she could remember, Gwen had been ridiculed by her family. It was a strong pattern, so she understood the fear of those who decided that perhaps she was actually a good person to know. They were scared of copping mockery themselves. Petra was too far gone to consider any such repercussions now, though. Gwen held her hand as her sister shared her heart.

A triangle of the road ahead was brightened by her bike light as Gwen rode home. She thought of her mother and how relieved she would be to see Gwen helping Petra.

She rested her foot on the road and waited at the red light. The street was deserted, with not a car in sight in either direction. She waited, regardless. There was no hurry and it was a balmy evening, perfect for a ride. A car came into view and pulled up on the opposite side of the intersection, triggering the lights to green. Gwen rode on, reflecting on the new family relationships evolving since her mother's death. It surprised her to be pleased about this, having grown so used to being alone in the family.

She rode past the town's main park and spotted

teenagers kissing under the distant lamplight. *Young love*, she thought: *so hopeful, ignorant and sweet*. The park gave way to large old houses. Gwen changed gears into an incline. Trees lined the street, trunks thick from decades of growth. She turned left and followed the descent holding her feet out off the pedals. She could feel the rush of evening air lifting her hair out behind her.

A pain ripped through her – she would never get to tell her mother about this night. Would she ever get used to her being dead, being gone forever, she wondered. She pulled over to catch her breath. Sitting on a lonely bench in front of shops lit low for the night, Gwen allowed her grief out – not that she could have stopped it. Grief was still the master. It called the shots and arrived whenever it liked.

There was no one around to see her sobbing. She wouldn't have noticed if they were. When her crying had finally dried up, she sat staring at the ground, numb. She heaved a sigh and mustered the energy to return to the evening by looking around her. Instead of riding home, she rode to the cemetery, lay on top of her mother's grave, oblivious to the cold concrete beneath her, and curled up as tight as she could. In that position, she fell asleep.

"Oh, I do like this purple chair," her new client Beatrice remarked. "Where on earth did you get it? I'll have to tell my friends about this one!"

"Yes, I love it too," Gwen replied. "I found it hidden in the back of a tiny antique store in an outback village. It was the most unexpected surprise. I bought it on the spot and shipped it back here. The original purple velvet was damaged beyond repair with dust and wear, so I had it reupholstered and brought it back to life."

"Yes, very nice, very nice," Beatrice replied, straightening her tartan skirt and adjusting the top button on her cardigan.

"So how can I help you today, Beatrice?"

"Well, it's a bit hard to admit, but my husband reckons I'm a troublemaker and need to stay out of other people's business."

"And what do you think?" Gwen asked kindly.

"Oh, I don't know. I just like to help people. Sometimes they make mistakes."

Gwen asked her what she considered mistakes. Beatrice mentioned that one of her neighbours lived alone and obviously needed to have more company. She had tried to tell her this, but the neighbour just kept shutting her down. Gwen pointed out that, in her experience, some people were genuinely happier on their own. Just because others lived differently, she said, didn't mean they were wrong.

"What's right for one person is not necessarily right for others."

"Yes, dear, when I hear that it makes sense. But when I'm with people, all I see is the mistake they're making, and I can't help trying to help them."

"Even if they haven't asked you to?"

"Well, yes. I've been guilty of that a time or two," Beatrice said.

"Do you have some kind of faith or belief in God?"

"Yes. I go to mass every Sunday without fail. I'm a good Christian woman."

"Do you think that you know better than God what each person is here to learn? Do you not think that perhaps each of the people you want to fix has their own lessons, ones that can only be mastered through the choices they're making for their own lives?"

Beatrice retreated into silence with a frown of consideration.

"Well, yes, dear, but some of them don't even go to church. Not any church!"

"Everyone has the right to choose their own beliefs," Gwen said gently. "Have you ever heard the saying, 'Let go. Let God'? It means to leave it up to God, not try solve it all yourself."

"Yes, and I'm starting to get your point. Maybe I *have* been a little interfering. One person recently called me self-righteous and I was deeply offended. But perhaps there's a *tiny* element of truth in it. Not that I'd admit it outside of this room."

Gwen smiled at her. "It's really just about respect, Beatrice. Respecting that we all have different lessons to learn here and what seems the right way for you isn't necessarily the right way for others."

"It's hard to imagine myself not helping people."

"OK, well, let's have a look at that then," Gwen said gently.

They spent the rest of the session looking at qualities Beatrice liked about herself, things that didn't involve trying to change or fix others. The idea was that she would focus on developing those qualities while learning to let go of the judgments and controlling behaviour. In time, Gwen assured her, those habits would learn to let go if Beatrice was truly willing to try. She had to be fully committed, though. She assured Gwen she was and booked her next appointment before offering a hug in farewell.

She was a back patter, Gwen noticed during the hug,

smiling over Beatrice's shoulder. Some clients held her in a desperate clutch. Some had little idea of how to relax in a hug until they let go into hers. Others gave great hugs that supported Gwen too. Some would have run if she even offered a hug. And then there were the back patters: those whose hands didn't hold the other person in an equal embrace but patted their back instead. She wasn't surprised that Beatrice was one. It was a nurturing habit and despite her interference, her intentions were kind.

Ten minutes after Beatrice had left, Gwen was at her desk doing some paperwork. She looked up to a slight tap on the door before it opened.

"Sorry to interrupt, dear," Beatrice said as her face peeked in. "I just wanted to say thank you again and what better way to do it than with cake? Here." She placed a whole chocolate gateau on Gwen's desk. "That should keep you going for a while. You can freeze some and bring it in each day, or you could share some with your friends, or ... Oh. I'm doing it again! Trying to organise people."

Gwen smiled and thanked her for the cake.

"You just enjoy that cake *however* you wish," Beatrice said and closed the door.

Gwen took the letter opener from the top drawer and cut a slice. As she licked the chocolate cream from her fingers afterwards, she couldn't help smiling. Life always seemed to know how to reward her when she needed it most.

Another week unfolded until there was no putting off the dinner date with Russ – unless life sent another gas leak on the road out of town. Gwen could only hope. Dread began filling her stomach as the day wore on. She knocked off work early and rode to the willow tree that she and her mother used to love.

Its branches were fully covered now in twisted leaves. Their subtle scent reached her before she was off her bike. As she lay the bike on the ground, she lifted a handful of leaves from near her feet and brought them to her nose. Tears immediately surfaced. She would always associate the smell with her mother.

She climbed in through the wall of leaves, leaned against the trunk and exhaled slowly. Allowing herself to settle into the space, she took a few more deep breaths and felt the dread, or the fear disguised as such, dissolve. Without words or articulated thought, she shared her feelings with her mother and felt her support, or what she would have offered. She would have said to relax and enjoy the night out with Russ. She would have said to let it just be fun and not overthink it, that Gwen deserved some lightness and lovely company. She would have encouraged her daughter to open her heart to possibilities without thinking too far ahead, and to take one step at a time.

Most of all, she would have reminded Gwen to let herself be surprised. Even with all that her mother had suffered, she still believed in the goodness of humanity and in hope. Gwen cried for missing her, smiling through the bittersweetness of the memories and wisdom, her heart aching with love.

She allowed the feelings to settle as the birds along the shallow river's edge below sang in glee. Her fingers collected dried leaves beside her and crumbled them unconsciously. It was time to be brave and open her heart a little. Her mother was right: she deserved some lightness and lovely company.

When her thoughts had been untangled and released, Gwen climbed back out from the cave of branches, brushed the leaves off her backside, looked up at the perfect, unbroken blue sky, and sent a prayer of thanks to her mother. Or God. Or whoever was guiding her. She smiled softly and rode towards home with a much lighter heart.

Relief was the first feeling, followed by enjoyment. Russ had chosen a different restaurant than where they had planned to meet the night of the gas leak, the night of meeting Declan.

She had looked this venue up on social media and while the meals looked tempting, it seemed a little too romantic for their first dinner. It wasn't. It had a fun atmosphere, without the need for trendy people to make it so. There was no 'in-crowd' feel, just happy folks all set for a night out. Gwen was one of those.

She made a quick but clear decision to be as present as possible, leaving no space for fears triggered by old experiences or imagined disasters. Doubts slinked off out the door within minutes, booted out by her determination to have an enjoyable night.

Russ was in complete gentleman mode and she allowed it. With his hand gently on the curve of her lower back, he guided Gwen to their table. Their conversation flowed naturally, as always, deepening with each story shared. She surprised herself by recalling and sharing crazy things she had done as a young adult – like going to a terrace house with a guy in Paris only to find out it was a brothel and that he was planning on putting her to work. She had gotten out of there very fast. She spoke of climbing trees as a girl and how she loved the privacy of being up there, away from the noise of family life. Even the dabbling in drugs she had done in her twenties was no longer a secret scandal.

For every story she shared, Russ matched her, but there was no fighting for attention between them. Instead, they absorbed each other's stories and were delighted or horrified by each other's experiences. Russ spoke about his father's disappointment in him for leaving the police force to open his own newsagency. He laughed, telling how he and his younger brother had accidentally set off a bomb in the family garage with a science experiment gone wrong. He spoke of tripping over on a train station platform in Sydney and getting his head stuck in the closing doors, and how all he could think of was how many different pairs of shoes were at his eye level. He had never run for a train again.

The various courses of the meal came and went, their flavours weaving silently through the stories. When the white cloth covering the table was left almost bare, and the last plates had been cleared by the waiter, Gwen felt sadness that the night was coming to a close. All that remained were their drinking glasses, a lit candle, and a small vase of flowers. Russ reached his hand over the space.

"Gwen. This has been the nicest experience I've had since I lost my wife and daughter. I never imagined I could feel anything for anyone again, but there's something very natural between us."

His hand remained on the table, waiting for hers, hidden in her lap. Her hesitation was brief before her courage lifted her hand to join his.

"I don't know what to say, Russ. I'm scared that words will get in the way. So I'm just going to say thank you for the loveliest night since my mum died. And yes, that's a good description: it is very natural between us." *But it won't stay lovely if we go deeper and get to know each other*, her fear ranted silently. *Oh, shut up*, courage interrupted. Gwen smiled and squeezed his hand.

The evening air was heavy with the scents of spring. The restaurant was down a little country lane, with few street lights. Stars were dotted above as they reached Gwen's car.

"I would have picked you up, you know?" Russ said. "Then our night wouldn't have to be over quite so fast. We could have shared drive time."

He touched her hair with such gentleness she almost moaned.

"I'm sure there'll be other opportunities," she replied in a quiet voice, allowing his touch while enjoying his eyes in the dimmed light of the carpark.

They licked their lips at the same and laughed shyly. His hand's touch on her face was too exquisite for any reply. He leaned in and kissed her once, then again, encouraged by her own response.

~

Claudia greeted her at the door, rubbing up against Gwen's leg as usual. "Hey, girl. How was your night?" She picked the cat up and sat out in her courtyard, looking at the night sky, thinking of her mum, and especially of the advice that her mother had often shared: to let herself be surprised. She was glad she had followed her mother's advice.

It took a while to get to sleep as memories of the evening floated through her mind, allowing Gwen to enjoy them all over again. She woke with a smile. Claudia ignored her as she did every morning. Not everything had changed.

5
———

AFTER THE KISS

Three days had gone by since Gwen and Russ had kissed. It had been years since she had kissed anyone. Well, anyone she actually knew and liked. She didn't count the strangers she'd had casual sex with. This was an actual kiss, with butterflies, a throbbing heart, nervousness, the whole thing. Three days and not a word.

As they parted, he had whispered that he would call the next day. Since he hadn't honoured that, there was no point in chasing him. His silence said enough.

Gwen tried to practice what she often taught her clients, people who came and sat in the purple chair in her clinic to offload their problems and untangle their thoughts. Try to be as mindful as possible, as present as you can, she would tell them.

Her mind seemed determined to obsess over his silence, though. It wasn't like him. Or was it? They had been friends for months and he seemed reliable, and yet he had kissed her and disappeared. She might have understood it if they had gone all the way. That might have been too much too soon for someone who had lost his wife only a few years ago. But a kiss and he ran. She couldn't wrap her head around it. She found herself fighting a constant battle with her thoughts, to take back whatever tiny bit of control she could to function in her life.

She felt like a desperate teenager with a crush on a boy who was more focused on playing it cool in front of his mates.

I could ring him, text him, visit him, she kept thinking, before reprimanding herself once more. Decades of life experience and she was back to being a teenager. It threatened to drive her quietly mad.

It was a beautiful morning as she rode her bicycle to work. She chose to focus on the clean air, gentle sunshine and the birds in their morning song. By the time she arrived at work, she had pedalled out most of her frustrations. With all the administration done before opening time, she lit a candle, watered the plants and then welcomed in her first client for the day.

"I lost my father when I was four," Maddy said. "He was there one minute, lifting me onto a branch and then climbing up to join me, or teaching me how to catch a ball. Though I wouldn't know, really – I was only four, after all. I'm not sure if they're my memories or things my mother told me. She said he was like that. A good bloke."

Gwen nodded. Maddy shifted her slight body further into the purple chair, shuffling her backside in as if she planned to stay a while. She lifted the back of her copper-coloured hair, which had settled into the collar of her floral blouse.

She took a breath and continued. "He died in a car crash. A drunk driver slammed into the side of his car at 8 am on a sunny morning. And just like that, he was dead and I was growing up without a father."

What if Russ is dead? Gwen thought. *That might explain it.* She took a sip of water and used the small break to bring her focus back to listening to her client.

"Mum was never with anyone else that I know of. She died when I was thirteen. It was sudden, just like my father. Way too young for a heart attack, but there you go. One minute she's hugging me off to school. The next I'm packing up everything I've known because that life is over. Forever. At least some of my memories of her are clearer. I still miss her, even though it's been ten years. I remember her more in feelings than in images."

Gwen gulped down the pain of losing her own mother. "I'm sorry to hear that, Maddy. That's a hard road you've been on."

"Oh well, it is what it is."

"So," Gwen said gently, "what's brought you here today? Obviously, all that affects everything you do, but is there anything specific I can support you with, or shall we just see what wants to come out?"

Morning light danced on the clinic floor through the swaying branches out the window. Maddy watched it for a moment, then looked up at Gwen.

"No. There's something specific. It's my aunt. I went to live with her and my uncle when my mother died. I grew up with my cousins, aged on both sides of me. It could have been worse, I guess. I could have ended up in foster care. At least I had some family. But now I'm 23 and I want to live as I want to, as my mother would have supported, but my aunt sees all my choices as wrong."

"Do you still live with her?"

"No way!" Maddy laughed. "I left two weeks after I turned 18, much to her disappointment. It doesn't matter what I do, though. I still disappoint her."

Maddy went on to explain that her mother had been highly creative. Most of her memories were of them doing things together like painting, dancing, sculpting, or creating pictures on the ground using leaves and twigs when they were out on bushwalks. Her aunt worked in the corporate sector and didn't support Maddy's choice to follow a creative path.

"Mum would just tell me to do what I want, I'm sure, and I am. But my aunt is sort of my replacement mother now and I hate going through life disappointing her. She won't get off my case either."

"Have you explained all this to her – that you feel your mother would approve of the choices you're making?"

"She won't let me talk about Mum. Never has. Says it's all behind us. She can't deal with anything painful. Just works herself into the ground and expects everyone else to do the same."

Gwen's heart ached for her. "Tell me about your mother," she said.

Maddy's face lit up and memories spilled out. She cried and laughed and cried some more, a wave of emotions woven through her stories. She remembered things she had forgotten, and realised she had already become much more like her mother than she knew.

"What would your mother do, Maddy?" Gwen asked as the stories came to an end.

"She'd do whatever she liked, but she'd also be kind in

explaining it to my aunt. She was a good person and really thoughtful of others. But she was also very clear and articulate. I remember that now. If she was guiding me or having to reprimand me, she was strong but fair, and always kind. And brave! I remember her standing up to an awful man in the market one day who was bullying her, trying to get in line first. She was definitely a brave woman."

Gwen smiled. "And you're your mother's daughter. I think you have your answer there on how to approach your aunt. With kindness, honesty and courage."

"Yes, I think that's it." Maddy looked down to the floor and appeared to be letting the conversation sink in.

"Life is a short and precious gift, Maddy. You of all people know the reality of that. So be kind, yes. But also, be that way with yourself. Don't let life pass you by while you're living according to someone else's expectations. I know you're not, but you're carrying guilt when there's no reason to. Do your best to explain to your aunt. But you're not responsible for her reaction from there. She is. She'll either push you away or learn to respect your choices."

The clock indicated the session was almost finished. Gwen began wrapping it up. Maddy stood and dusted down her skirt. "I'm going to keep making my mum proud." She shook Gwen's hand with a smile of thanks and gathered her handbag.

"I think you're right, Maddy," Gwen replied in farewell, "but make *you* proud too. It's *your* life. Keep choosing it well."

"I might come back and chat again, Gwen. This has been good. But there's a lot to absorb now, so I might let that sink in first."

It was time for lunch with "the girls", a cluster of self-employed women who found great cheer in supporting each other in business and life by getting together once a month. Susan, the newest member of the group, had unknowingly chosen Gwen's favourite café in town for lunch. Gwen's niece, who worked there, was their waitress. Gwen winked at Samantha in greeting as she began taking their orders.

A year ago, Samantha had been like the rest of Gwen's family: judgmental towards her, critical and mean. She was proud of the young woman Samantha was becoming, with the courage to step out of that awful family mould and be pulled forward by curiosity instead. When Samantha had approached her, wanting to get to know her better, Gwen had been astounded but secretly delighted.

With honesty and a love of cooking, their friendship was deepening all the time. She was grateful to enjoy the family bond, that strange sense of connection through blood and the understanding of family dysfunction. Gwen thought, for her clients too, that family often meant being bonded by secrets. Only family members usually accepted others' bad behaviour for as long as they did.

She was grateful to have stopped accepting her own family's bad behaviour, but it didn't necessarily make it easier, particularly at family functions. One small blessing with her mother now dead was that there were fewer occasions to endure.

"Here you go, Auntie Gwen. Your salmon salad." Samantha placed the plate down.

"Thank you, sweetheart. But I think it's time we dropped

the 'Auntie' before my name. You're an adult now and I'm not exactly an old spinster aunt." Samantha pulled a funny face assessing whether the 'old' was true or not and everyone laughed.

The connection with these women was vital for Gwen's well-being. Working for herself was a choice she was grateful to have, and she loved it, but spending time with others who also worked for themselves was good for her soul. The gaggle of chatter and humour was a whirlwind in any venue they visited, but what proprietor could resist a table of laughter and women spending on their tax accounts? It was a work meeting, after all.

An afternoon storm arrived not long before Gwen was due to ride home, but passed in the nick of time. Everything was washed clean and she smiled to see it, especially once she turned into her own tree-lined street and noticed all the leaves so fresh and shiny.

Gwen's cat Claudia was an independent creature, but usually greeted her by rubbing against her leg when the door opened. Last night, though, when Gwen had arrived home, Claudia had looked up from her cushion briefly and gone back to sleep. The next morning she had seemed her normal self, eating some of the food she had left in her bowl the night before. When she had finished, Gwen had picked her up and given her a tender cuddle. Claudia purred in response. Gwen had put her down and smiled as she received a rub against her leg in reply. She had straightened up Claudia's cushion and blanket, and left for work.

When she opened the door tonight, the first thing she noticed was no dent in the cat's favourite cushion by the sunny window. She looked down to a blank space instead of the familiar rub against her leg. Her stomach sank as she dropped her handbag and walked through her small home calling for Claudia, checking all of her favourite spots first.

It was the tail she noticed first, a glimpse of it under the bed.

"Oh, Claudia." She rushed down to her to offer comfort but it was too late. Her cat had left the world. "No, sweetie, no," Gwen whispered, delicately bringing the stiff body out into view. "Oh, Claudia," she said as the tears came. She sat against the bed, the dead cat by her side on the soft carpet. She looked at the little body beside her and howled in grief: for her cat, for her mother, and for herself. Sobs rocked her body, then eased only to start again.

When Gwen was finally drained and sat there empty, staring at the soft pink wall, a problem presented itself. She couldn't throw Claudia into a rubbish bin. Nor could she bury her in the compact paved courtyard of her little home. She thought of some of her siblings with backyards, but couldn't bear to ask them if she could bury Claudia there. She would never be at peace leaving her pet there either.

The only person she could think of who might help was her younger sister, Petra, who had reached out to Gwen recently for help and was beginning to show a little humanity.

~

It was a hot night after the rain. At least it made the

ground soft, Gwen thought. Mosquitoes buzzed around her, her sister and her niece. She hardly noticed. Samantha had bought a small rose bush to go into Petra's garden over Claudia. Her sister had also shown more compassion than Gwen knew her to be capable of, buying two bunches of flowers before Gwen had arrived with Claudia wrapped in her favourite blanket.

"One bunch is for you and one is for us to put in Claudia's grave with her."

Gwen hugged her sister in thanks through tears.

"I'm sorry I didn't know her, Gwen. The cat, I mean. There's so much about your life I don't know about."

"Thanks, Petra."

"No, I'm serious," her sister said.

"Well, and this isn't an attack," Gwen said to soften the oncoming honesty, "you've never shown interest or asked me anything."

"I know," Petra replied. "I know." She put her arm around her. "Come on. Let's bury this cat of yours. She was sweet, you said?"

Gwen smiled in memory. "When she wanted to be. She was a cat. She called the shots."

With Claudia wrapped in her blanket in the damp ground, the three women separated flowers from the bunch and dropped them into the hole. Raindrops began to spatter lightly. Gwen hated to think of the blanket being wet and Claudia being cold. Her sob came from nowhere.

"Let's get this covered up before the sky really opens," Petra said.

Her clothes drenched, Gwen declined the offer of a cup of tea. She drove home, numb to the rhythm of the windscreen wipers.

~

He had a big laugh for a little man, and a big voice, both facts that took Gwen by surprise as she shook hands with Felix, before gesturing to the purple chair. He laughed easily and she liked him instantly. He reminded her of someone who would live in the woods in Scandinavia, with strong arms, skin unblemished by the harsh Australian sun, and wearing boots that had already seen many years outdoors.

"How can I help you?" Gwen asked once they were both settled. It was midday and she had snuck a cookie in before the session to avoid her belly rumbling midway through. This was her last session before lunch. Cookies had become a regular item in her top drawer. Just one per day. Today's had been a disgustingly wonderful honeycomb one.

The window was open slightly and the breeze caressed her cheek. She smiled at Felix and brushed a last tiny crumb from her mouth.

"Well," he said, and laughed, "it seems I laugh too much." The pain behind his laughter surfaced in a frown. "That's what my wife tells me, anyway."

"Oh, that's a sad accusation," Gwen remarked. "I'd hate to see that fabulous laugh of yours silenced. I've only known you for a few minutes and it's already lifted my spirits. What's going on, Felix? Why did she say that?"

He said it seemed to be one of those textbook cases where the thing that attracted someone eventually became the thing that repelled them. "She's from a quiet family," he added. "Her father hardly says a word."

His wife had been drawn to his big laugh. For the first ten years of their marriage, she would smile almost every time he did, sometimes even chuckling along with him.

"Then one day," Felix said, "she just snapped and said, 'Why do you have to laugh so much?' Well, it threw me off completely! I'd always been like that, so her reaction hit me out of the blue. Since then, I've felt like I'm walking on eggshells the whole time. And when we visit her parents, it's worse. She used to laugh with me, but now she rolls her eyes with her father. I've got no idea what I did wrong, or how to fix it. I feel like I'm the same person I always was with her."

"And you've tried to talk with her about it?"

"Sure have. She says she still likes that I laugh, but just doesn't want to hear it all the time. How am I supposed to know when's the right or wrong time? It hardly makes for spontaneous laughter, does it?"

"No, Felix, it doesn't."

"Then, because I'm feeling so sensitive about it all and have quietened down a bit, she accused me of not laughing much at all anymore. Damned if I do, damned if I don't!"

"Oh dear."

"Yes," he agreed. "And this has been going on for almost a year now. I come from a laughing family. We laugh often, without thinking. We have fun together. It's just who I am. And after a year of treading delicately, I'm exhausted."

"Yes, it certainly would be exhausting trying to be someone you're not. No wonder you're feeling that way. So the question is, can you talk about it with her, to try to get to the root of it?"

He shook his head. "No, she's not ready for that yet, but she has a counselling session next week. Not with you. A different name, it was. I suggested we do a session together with someone, but she said I need to look at myself first." He took a sip of water and watched a small bird flitting about just outside the window.

His pain was real, but as far as Gwen could ascertain by the end of their time, he was a devoted husband and a good human. There was no way of her knowing both sides of the story but saw there was some work as a couple ahead if they were to stay together.

As they said goodbye at the door, he turned back to Gwen. "I simply have to laugh my way through life sometimes. It can be hard or it can be joyful. And sometimes it's a bit of both, but without laughter – no, that's not living at all."

Occasionally, Gwen found herself recalling remarks and stories her clients had shared. She benefitted from some sessions as much as they did. The final comment from Felix was one such time. When she thought about who she enjoyed laughing with, Russ came to mind. They laughed easily together even though both were dealing with the individual losses of people they loved.

It had been almost two weeks and she still hadn't heard from him.

It was Tuesday afternoon, Gwen's time off each week to indulge in whatever enjoyment she felt called to. It wasn't enjoyable driving to his newsagency, wondering if he would reject her on sight, but since she was done with the silence there seemed little choice. She needed to see his face, which would tell her more than his voice on the phone or a texted reply.

It was a large store, extending deep back from the street, selling stationery and magazines, gifts and computer parts. Gwen wandered slowly through all the aisles, hoping for a glimpse of him. A young employee noticed her and asked if she needed anything.

"No, thank you. Just browsing," she lied to the woman and soon walked out of the store. It was just up the street from here that she and Russ had met. Gwen had just walked out of a café, after a slice of delicious hummingbird cake and two strong coffees, when a teenager's skateboard had escaped him, stopping at her head. Russ, with his floppy hair and caring nature, had been one of her first sights as she looked up from the ground.

Her feet found their way to the same café. She took a seat by the window. Plenty of people were out and about, but there was no sign of Russ. She ordered a piece of chocolate cake and a strong coffee. The cake was divine: moist, sweet, but not overly so.

To return to her car she either had to walk back past the newsagency or right around the block to avoid it. She wanted to see him, but also to reject him before he rejected her. *He's already won on that account*, Gwen reminded herself. *He hasn't called when he said he would*. Not knowing why drove her crazier than the actual rejection. She walked back into his store. The woman looked up from behind the counter. "Hi ... again! I'll leave you to browse. Please let me know if I can help."

"Actually, you can," Gwen said. "Is Russ about?"

"Oh. No, he's not. Are you a friend of his?"

"Yes, and I've not heard from him for a while, which is unusual."

The woman's face made it plain there was bad news.

"I'm sorry, but Russ was in an accident."

Gwen was surprised by her own tears. Whether relief that it wasn't rejection or concern for him, she couldn't tell. She wiped them away.

"What happened? Is he OK?"

The woman shook her head. "He's alive, but not really OK."

He had been slammed into by a truck on the way home from their dinner. The truck driver had died instantly, with too many drugs in his system for anywhere near safe driving. The car Russ had been driving was damaged beyond repair. One arm had been shattered, and he had received a nasty concussion. Doctors had put him into an induced coma to help monitor his brain health.

"His sister came to town and dropped in to let us know. None of us staff have been able to see him yet. But she came in yesterday and apparently he's out of the coma. A bit groggy, but he was able to talk with her a little."

Gwen nodded in shock.

"You're not Gwen, are you?"

"Yes," she smiled. "Why?"

"His sister asked me yesterday, 'Who the hell is Gwen?'. I told her I had no idea."

A sob escaped Gwen. She put her hand on the counter to steady herself.

"Apparently," the woman continued, "your name was the first thing he said when he came back to consciousness. His sister thought he was talking gibberish, but he asked after you again yesterday morning."

"I need her number. Please."

"I don't have it, but I do know he can't have any visitors yet, except for family. She's been dropping in every few days, so how about you give me your number and she can call you?"

Since it seemed her only choice, Gwen wrote her number down. She thanked the young woman and drove back to Wattledale in a daze. She didn't notice the paddocks of golden wheat, huge puffy clouds floating through the gorgeous blue sky, or the flock of white cockatoos squawking around a large tree near the side of the road.

He hadn't ghosted her. There was no rejection. How crazy the mind could be, she thought. How capable we are of driving ourselves crazy, based on ignorant assumptions about another.

There was nothing she could do but wait and pray that he would be OK. Gwen realised that it would affect her very much if he died, not just because it would be another death to deal with. It was time to stop denying her feelings: Russ mattered.

~

Lan sat in the purple chair and smoothed down the velvet on its arms. Gwen watched as her client noticed the chandelier above her, the plants by the window, and the large flower photo framed on the wall. Lan's jet-black hair shone even without sunlight upon it. Her tiny body seemed even smaller in the purple chair. When she finished her observation of the room, she nodded with a quiet smile and then turned back to Gwen.

"Nice space."

"Thanks," Gwen replied. "So how can I support you today, Lan?"

"I thought it was interesting that you call yourself a listener. Someone I work with told me about it, and then I saw it on your door."

"Yes. I felt it fitted me more honestly than 'psychologist' or 'counsellor', though I'm qualified as those. Calling myself a listener feels more comfortable for me, and I think for a lot of my clients too. I think listening's a lost art and is underestimated."

"Funny you say that," Lan said, "because I'm tired of listening. That's why I'm here. I'm tired of being a dumping ground for people who won't even take an honest look at themselves."

"Yes, it can take a lot of courage for people to do that, and to own the consequences of their actions."

Lan explained that her brother complained to her all the time about his neighbour, saying the neighbour was toxic and always causing drama and problems. Yet the amount of time her brother spent complaining about the neighbour was almost as destructive as the neighbour's words and actions. It had started to drain her so much she was considering spending less time around him.

"And you've asked him to lay off from talking about the neighbour so much?"

"Absolutely. But he's addicted to it. I'm starting to wonder if the neighbour moved, whether my brother wouldn't just create a new drama around someone else. He's free to choose his own life. I don't care what he does, but I do care that he expects me to be his dumping ground and listen to it all on repeat."

"Yes, it's a pity that some people are so addicted to their patterns that they can't even see them. It's even more of a pity when you try to speak honestly and it does no good, and all you can do is avoid the person."

"It's not like the clock ticks any slower for me than him. My time's just as important. Listening to him go on and on about his neighbour isn't how I want to spend my time. It not only drains me but also takes me away from things I enjoy."

"Have you tried distracting him when he brings up the neighbour, like changing the topic?"

"I sure have, and he returns to it almost immediately."

"What about ending the conversation as soon as he raises it?"

'I've tried that one too."

"OK," Gwen said before letting the silence sit for a moment. "What did you hope to achieve from our session today then, Lan, besides you not being the listener for a change?"

"Good question. I suppose if I'm really honest, I just needed you to validate that I've done all I could. This will justify my walking away from my brother for a while, without wondering if there was more I could do. There's not. He'll just find some other sucker to listen to his whinging, I'm sure. But at least it won't be me." She paused, then took a deep breath. "I'm so exhausted, Gwen, and I just wish he could see what he's doing."

"Not everyone's ready or brave enough to look within, Lan. People can be scared of what they might find. You've clearly done some inner work, so you know how confronting it can be to break old patterns and be honest with yourself. Not everyone has the strength to do it."

"Not everyone has the balls to, more like," she replied.

"Not that either. So your decision is made?"

Lan said it was. She accepted that she needed to create some space between her and her brother's dramas. It was time to be around people who left her feeling inspired rather than exhausted. She would put more effort into her friendships and take a break from visiting him for a while.

"I'm scared, though," she said, pausing at the door on her way out. "What if he dies while I'm having a break? I don't know that I could live with the guilt."

Gwen looked seriously at her. "What if *you* die? Is being a doormat how you'd want to be living your last chapter?"

Lan nodded slowly, taking it in. "Good point. OK," she frowned, looking down to the floor and then back up to Gwen. "Actually ... actually, Gwen, I don't think I can do this. A part of me wants to and I know it makes sense to, but I don't think I can abandon him."

"What about *your* happiness, Lan?"

Lan wiped away a tear and shrugged. A sad smile rose briefly and was gone. She pulled the door closed behind her.

∼

The summer sky was enormous and clear. Gwen didn't feel like going home, particularly since her cat was no longer there. Instead, she rode towards the cemetery. Just before reaching it, she changed direction and headed to the willow tree on the other side of town. The essence of her mother was stronger at the tree they used to meet under than at a concrete slab at a cemetery.

As she rode closer to the tree, she was shocked to see her sister's car parked nearby. Petra had never spent time with their mother here. It was a place that only Gwen held memories of. She pulled up and lay the bike down upon a mattress of dead leaves.

"Petra?"

She heard the rustle behind the wall of branches and her sister's head poked out. "Gwen! Hi! Is this the one? Is this the tree Mum used to come to?"

Gwen could only nod.

"Samantha told me about it. Please don't be mad I'm here. I just felt I had to talk with Mum."

Gwen climbed into the cave of leaves and sat beside her.

"I've never talked out loud to Mum since she died," Petra said, "so I came here to apologise."

Her sister's red eyes told Gwen she had done more than that.

"I was such a selfish daughter. I never really put myself in her shoes. It must have been really hard with all of us kids. Samantha said she never got over Dad leaving, either."

"That's true. I told Samantha that. I figured if even just one niece knew the truth, then at least someone in the next generation would know Mum better, if only as a memory."

Petra nodded. Her steady stream of tears continued to fall. "I've got so many regrets around Mum, Gwen. I never knew her as a person, as a woman. Just as a mother, and even then I didn't treat her with much gratitude or love."

Gwen told her it was OK. Her mother understood the influence their father and his opinions had had on them all. "She knew you were a good person, Petra."

"Do you think?" her sister sniffled. Gwen nodded with a smile, then put her arms around Petra, holding her while the tears continued. The wall of leaves swayed gently around them, cocooning them from the world.

Petra pulled back from the hug and looked at Gwen. "How do I ever forgive myself?"

"You need to have some compassion for yourself. You did your best as who you were at the time. Now you can see things you would have done differently. So how about trying compassion for your old self from your current self? Mum understood. It didn't stop her from loving you."

Her sister's renewed sobs fell onto Gwen's shoulders. "How could she love me? I was so thoughtless and unkind."

"She still loved you. Don't worry, she definitely did."

The ache in Gwen's heart for her mother was almost unbearable. It had barely lessened since their mother had died. While Gwen missed her terribly, she was grateful too. There were no regrets. She had been a kind, thoughtful daughter and had carried her mother through some of her hardest times, just as her mother had done for Gwen in her younger years. She missed the friendship they shared more than anything, the laughter under this tree, the honesty and the love.

When Petra's tears had fully dried, they lay on the soft cushioning of dried leaves, looked at the roof of the green ones above, and talked as they never had before. Gwen shared stories about her mother, and Petra about herself. The comfort of watching the leaves swing softly, the swish of their rhythm with the river's song in the background, opened their hearts in safety. The stories flowed until the sun was almost gone for the day.

They said goodbye beside Gwen's bike. Petra dusted a leaf off Gwen's shoulder. Gwen took one from Petra's hair.

She rode home, exhausted in a good way. The final colours of sunset lit the sky behind. It felt like a day well-lived.

Gwen was with a client when the phone message came in. Emotions rushed through her when she listened to it later. Russ was finally allowed visitors outside of his family, but only during visiting hours. It was Friday, and her work day was full, which meant she couldn't visit him today. She would see him the next morning.

She woke earlier than expected, still unused to Claudia's absence. There were no paws massaging the quilt, no purrs echoing through the bedroom. She tried to read but couldn't focus, so rose and followed a morning qi gong session online. A tease of sunrise hit the front of her home. She squinted through the screen, trying to force the day's arrival with impatience.

With a craving for ginger, she juiced some, along with carrots and oranges. Gwen never tired of the feeling of nourishment sliding down her throat.

A little later, clothes covered her bed, indecision piling high. She stopped at the eighth outfit. It would have to do. The visiting hours would be over if Gwen was waiting to feel comfortable in what she wore. The navy flowing dress was one of her favourites anyway. After three changes of accessories, she settled for a long string of beads. The bright orange sat well against the dark background. Slipping on orange and magenta sandals completed the outfit. The decision to change her handbag wasn't made until she had locked the front door. With a sigh, she unlocked it, emptied the contents of her black bag onto her bed, still covered in clothes, and moved them into a funky little orange bag. With a quick roll of an essential oil perfume blend against her neck and wrists, she was done.

She didn't notice the absence of music on the drive. *Was he OK? Were her feelings real or just confused by his initial silence? What if she cried? What if she peed herself?* (She was nervous enough to.) *What would she say? What would they talk about? Breathe, Gwen. Just breathe.* She followed her own silent instructions. A third long exhale finally brought her back to earth. She found a parking spot and pulled in.

"Hello, you," Russ said gently as she entered the hospital room, his smile breaking into a beam of happiness.

"Hi, yourself," Gwen replied, suddenly shy. She walked to the side of his bed. They had kissed that night, but a hug now felt too personal. Noticing her hesitation, he took her hand and squeezed it. Stitches came down from his hairline, mending a cut on the side of his forehead. His other hand and arm were in a plaster cast.

"How are you feeling?" she asked.

"Better for seeing you."

She chose silence as a safer reply than whatever might spew from her madness, and looked down at the floor.

"Gwen," Russ said.

She raised her head in reply.

"Look, I know it's only been a kiss, but I've had a lot of time to think. We're adults. We both know how suddenly good things can change. I'm not willing to waste time. I need you to know that the thought of your smile has been the beacon of my recovery here."

Gwen's eyes became a little watery as she gulped down the pain of love. And it was love, she realised. All she could do was smile and let her eyes spill. She wiped some tears away, unable to speak.

"Come here," his gentle voice invited, and he held his working arm out. She leaned into his one-sided hug, inhaling his scent of masculinity.

He released his hold and then looked into her eyes. "Bring the chair closer, Gwen. I need you close." Her smile broadened as she nodded.

∾

Gwen found the observation of her own thoughts fascinating. Life on the outside was the same in most ways. She worked and enjoyed time with her clients, her business friends, her niece and even her sister. There was grocery shopping to do and weeds to be pulled from the potted plants in her courtyard. She cleaned her car as usual. It was when she found herself giving her bike a thorough clean that she realised she was high in love. The battle of resistance was gone. She was willing to fall into whatever it would become with Russ. She realised how much energy had gone into keeping herself safe from the potential pain of love. She had long forgotten the *good* side of it.

Life felt easier and more flowing. People remarked on how well she looked when all that had changed were her mindset and the cracking open of her heart.

As she walked down the street in Wattledale, lost in a daydream, with a quiet smile, a familiar voice said hello in an unfamiliar tone. She stopped and saw the face of one of her older brothers. It was Samantha's father.

"Oh, hi, Mark. How are you?"

"I'm OK," he replied. "How are you, Gwen?"

He had *never* asked her that. Not even once. She stammered in surprise.

"Uh, yeah, good, yes. I'm doing well, thanks, Mark. What's happening in your world?"

"Oh, I'm just filling in time waiting for the car to be serviced. I had a couple of beers at the pub but after lunch it was just me and the old, bored guys. So I thought I'd go for a walk instead, and here you are."

Gwen waited for the sarcasm, the criticism masked in jokes or even the direct insult. She knew how to handle all that. But this – this was new. Her brother was speaking with her like an adult, and a respectful one at that.

"Samantha tells me you two have become friends."

"We have. And we've been cooking some of Mum's recipes together."

"I don't suppose you've made her tropical fruit pie yet, have you?"

Gwen shook her head with a smile. "No. Not yet."

An unexpected rush of care for him flooded her heart. "Uh, would you like us to make you one sometime?"

He didn't look away fast enough for Gwen to miss the single tear. He wiped it away, less discreetly than intended. "Sure, Gwen. I'd like that. I can't imagine anyone could make it as well as Mum used to, but I'm willing to try it. I'm sure I'll survive your and Samantha's cooking."

"It's a deal," she said, and laughed. "The only condition is that you come and eat it with Samantha and me at my place. We're catching up on Saturday afternoon. How's that for you?"

"OK," he agreed with a smile.

"Or better still, you can help us cook it."

"Oh! Ah, OK. I'm up for trying."

"Great! See you soon, then."

"Yep, sure will. Bye, Gwen."

She walked away from their farewell in shock. Her brother had never treated her with anything close to respect, let alone interest. She shook her head in amazement and climbed the stairs to her clinic.

Sitting in the purple chair, a sense of wonder filled her heart. Life was certainly full of surprises. She realised it always could have been. Her heart had just been too closed.

She thought of her mother and though her heart still ached, she smiled. Yes, life was certainly an interesting ride, if you were willing to get fully on board. Her mother would be enjoying all this, wherever she was. Gwen rested her head against the high back of the purple chair and acknowledged that she too was enjoying it all. She shook her head and laughed.

6

THE TENDER HEART

A chill in the air hinted at autumn's return. Summer held on, but the subtle shift brought ease. It had been a scorching season, with roads shimmering in the constant heat and folks staying indoors through the midday hours. Gwen had escaped much of it in her air-conditioned clinic. In autumn, she could turn that off and let fresh air flow through.

She looked around her room. The touches of colour and the plants had transformed it into a safe haven for so many. The purple chair with its high back and smooth velvet was a well-loved feature, but the flavour of the room was based more on subtleties than the obvious.

Plants sat in quirky pots against the sunniest wall and under the window. A print of flowers adorned another wall and a chandelier hung from the ceiling. The tiny spider who had dwelled there had moved on. Gwen wondered if it would return in another season, perhaps for the warmth of the room in winter when wood burned every day in the old blue-tiled fireplace. Her clinic room almost felt like home.

She had occasionally wondered if that was why her clients were so comfortable sharing as openly as they did.

A candle burned most of the day, its scent filling the room. Lemongrass seemed a favourite for most. Gwen's own choice would have been frangipani or jasmine – their sweet flowery aromas lifted her mood every time – but the setting wasn't about her. The people who sat in the purple chair and trusted her at their most vulnerable were the priority. Many had commented on the lemongrass scent when it wafted through the room. She unpacked two dozen new candles into the vintage cabinet.

As she sat in silence in the purple chair, looking around her workspace, an unexpected decision arrived: it was time to cut down on her working hours. Gwen already took Tuesday afternoons and every weekend off, but a yearning from nowhere insisted on more. The waiting list for her services as a listener was constant. Despite there being other counsellors and psychologists in the area, Gwen's list was always full. Yet the call to work less was undeniable. People would wait, or go elsewhere.

The soft tones of afternoon sunlight announced the drawing in of the day. Gwen remained in the purple chair, contemplating what cutting back her work hours truly meant. She smiled when the realisation hit: it was time to put herself first.

Since her mother's death almost two years ago, she had worked her usual hours, supporting her clients. She was always looking after someone, in one capacity or another. It was now time to look after herself as well.

Russ brought the food, and Gwen provided the juice, picnic blanket and eating utensils. It was his first outing since the car accident that had sent him to the hospital with a concussion and shattered arm. His head was fine and his arm was healing, but it was still very tender.

Gwen knew a couple of great spots elsewhere, but both held memories she didn't want to overlap with new ones. One was a willow tree she had often shared with her mother before she died. It stood beside a shallow river and would still have shade and privacy for another couple of weeks. Then the leaves would start changing and dropping. By the end of autumn, its branches would be bare sticks blowing in the breeze.

Another ideal picnic spot was the green riverbank she had shared a leisurely afternoon by, making love with a stranger in his campervan. She didn't need to bring such a memory into the picnic with Russ, so was happy to leave the decision with him.

She hadn't known of the little dirt track that led to the delightful creek that now meandered past them. Its pure water bubbled over clean stones, worn smooth over eons. By the look of the track coming in through the bushland, it was a secret place and rarely visited.

A grassed area captured gentle sunshine, dappled with a little shade. They lay the blanket down and unpacked the food, drinks and utensils from the cooler bag and basket. Sitting on the blanket, they loaded each other's plates in a team effort. Russ spotted a shy wallaby before it hopped off into the bushland. Birdsong welcomed them from all directions.

Kisses interrupted their eating and chatter until one of them pulled back. Then they ate some more, kissed again, talked a bit, kissed some more, and pulled back again. The anticipation was unbearable. Gwen had not ached with such longing for anyone for ... she couldn't remember how long, if she ever had. She had to have him, yet he insisted today was not the day. He was too scared of injuring his arm. She was tempted to mount him anyway, or at least offer to, but it was clear he needed their first time to be right for him too. So they kissed like teenagers: aching, longing, resisting. At least the food was satisfying.

Kelsey wore a bright floral dress, one more geared towards spring than this cloudy day somewhere between summer and autumn. It accentuated her smooth dark skin beautifully. She unwrapped a sky-blue shawl from her shoulders, folded it and draped it over the handbag at her feet. She had clearly felt at home quickly and was speaking within seconds of sitting down in the purple chair.

"I'm so over money. That's it! That's why I'm here. I won't say I hate money, because I need it, but there just never seems to be enough. I feel really restricted by it."

"Yes," Gwen said, "having money gives you choices and not having it – well, you're right, it *is* restrictive. So tell me, what's happening at the moment for you?"

"Well," Kelsey replied with a sigh, "I work and work, sometimes two jobs, and never seem to get anywhere. Even if I work longer hours, I still somehow never end up with extra money."

While listening, Gwen noticed the stunning, blue, high-heeled sandals that Kelsey wore. Kelsey noticed her looking and smiled.

"Nice shoes," Gwen said.

"Thanks. I bought this outfit to match them because I loved them so much and couldn't find anything in my wardrobe to do them justice."

"Well, you succeeded. You look fabulous."

"Thanks, Gwen!"

"Do you have many other fabulous pairs of shoes?"

Kelsey moved her feet under the chair. "Oh, too many, I imagine. But shoes and clothes are what make me happy. I feel good when I'm wearing nice clothes."

"You have great style, I'll give you that," Gwen said. "But if you're going to solve this money issue, you have to be honest with yourself. How many pairs of shoes do you own?"

"I don't know. At least fifty, I guess ... maybe sixty ... maybe more?" Kelsey tried to laugh it off.

Gwen waited a moment and then asked, "How many would you say you wore at least every fortnight?"

"About five or six, but I wear the others for special occasions."

"Even the uncomfortable ones?"

"Even those."

The women laughed gently with each other.

"OK," Gwen said, "I think a good first step to healing your relationship with money is for us to look at what emptiness new clothes and shoes are really filling for you."

"Wow," Kelsey said with a smile. "I didn't expect to be talking about shoes! But I hear you and I'm willing."

Under Gwen's instruction, Kelsey began writing down all the feelings she enjoyed when buying new clothes and shoes, and then wearing them. Halfway down the page, she paused. "This list also reminds me of how proud I used to feel when Dad liked what I was wearing," she said with a smile. Gwen nodded and guided her to also write down her feelings of guilt, regret or anger at herself that followed such purchases.

They proceeded into a guided meditation during which Gwen created space for Kelsey to remember the times she had felt most loved by her father as a child. In each of these memories, Kelsey had been dressed in her finest clothes, never her casual, play clothes. Kelsey's father had only paid her attention when she was dressed up prettily for when his friends came to visit – when she represented the perfect daughter. Kelsey came out of the meditation in tears.

"Oh, my goodness, Gwen. I thought this was about me spending too much, but it's so much more. I almost wish I hadn't opened this can of worms."

"Things are rarely as they seem. There's something deeper beneath every habit, a driving force. Once you dare to look that honestly, you come to realise how much it weighs you down. There's a better life waiting for you, Kelsey."

Gwen reminded her that it was a step-by-step process and that change is often subtle but powerful. They formulated a plan for Kelsey to make some money in the meantime by holding a stall at an upcoming regional market. She would sell the clothes she rarely wore, items that actually left her feeling worse about herself.

"Some of them are really uncomfortable, to be honest," Kelsey admitted. "One pair of checked green trousers goes up my bum crack every time, no matter which knickers I wear underneath. I have to wear a jacket that covers my behind. It's time *they* went!"

Gwen laughed with her.

"Actually," Kelsey continued, "I really like *your* style, Gwen, and I bet you don't spend a fortune."

"I like quality, definitely, not quantity," Gwen said, "and I've mastered the whole mix-and-match thing. But this isn't about my wardrobe as much as realising you're already enough, Kelsey, even without new clothes to be admired in. You're a good person and just because your father was unable to love you as you needed doesn't mean you can't try to love yourself. The journey to self-love takes a lot of courage and many conscious choices, but I believe you can do it. And you'll very likely change your money story in the process."

One of the things Gwen had savoured in single life was not answering to anyone. She understood why Russ asked about her day – he was keen to know her better in these early days of love. If only she could find a way to share information that felt comfortable. For the moment, she ignored his name on the ringing phone, put it in her bag and locked up the clinic for the day.

"Another day, another dollar, hey Gwen?" Bert from the hobby shop downstairs said as she unlocked her bike from the rack.

"You got it, Bert, you got it," she replied with a smile. It was a simple greeting, but one of those rituals in daily life that brought unexpected pleasure. She thought about those routines that creep into people's lives unnoticed, yet play a sweet role in them. Greeting Bert most afternoons was one of them, as was watching him stroll off up the path.

Gwen's phone rang again. By the time she took her bag from her back and found the phone, the call had been missed. It was Russ again. She turned the phone off completely, dropped it in her bag, secured the bag to her back again and rode down the street.

At the block before her turnoff to home, she turned left instead of right. The longing for her mother was unbearable. She would have known what to say to Gwen, to help her ease the struggle around Russ and his daily phone calls.

She wasn't there, though. She was dead. Gwen wondered if the pain would ever lessen. She rode towards her mother's old house, long sold to new owners. The ride through the familiar neighbourhood was a comfort at least. There was no point stopping in front of the house and alerting old nosy neighbours. She slowed and rolled by, happy to see her mother's rose bush still in the front yard.

It had taken her a long time to recognise how much clarity bike riding brought her. As her legs circled, her hands steered and the breeze blew softly into her face, she considered how adults are still children if their parents are alive, whether they like it or not. It didn't matter if they were close, either.

But there was no mother to be the daughter of anymore and it ripped at Gwen's heart. Tears rolled down her cheeks and were dried by the early evening breeze. She was tempted to ride out to the willow tree on the other side of town, but could only set herself up for so much pain in one night. Instead, she headed for home.

There was no point turning on the lights in the darkened space. She knew her way and easily found her mother's old shirt, held it tightly, curled into a ball on the floor, and sobbed into the emptiness.

～

It was a rainy afternoon when Gwen opened the door to Samantha and her father, Mark. She greeted them both and beckoned them in, took their umbrella and leant it under the eaves outside in a dry spot.

"OK," her niece said, rubbing her hands together. "Let's get cooking!"

"I don't know why I had to be here for the actual cooking, Gwen," Mark said as he followed them to the kitchen. "I just want to taste something like Mum used to cook, not actually cook it."

Gwen smiled. Always resistance. It was how her family worked. "Well, brother, I'm not your slave and if you want something in life, you have to take some action yourself sometimes."

He was clearly unimpressed, but Gwen no longer cared what he thought. Same for most of her siblings. That indifference and lack of need for acceptance allowed her a new freedom of expression. She no longer had to keep the peace for her mother's sake.

"Do you want to eat some tropical fruit pie later or not? Pretty simple, really."

Mark exhaled loudly, shook his head with annoyance, and gave in. "Yeah, OK, where do I start?"

"Right, Dad," Samantha chipped in. "You and I can start with the pastry for the base. Grab the flour, butter, sugar and an egg. You're stronger than me so you'll make a good pastry roller. Here!" She threw the wooden rolling pin to him.

He smiled, put it on the bench, rolled up his sleeves,

washed his hands in the kitchen sink, and said, "OK, then. Let's do this!"

Gwen didn't ask about his preference for music. Cooking pie automatically called for George Jones or Patsy Cline. It was all their mother had cooked to. She chose George Jones and noticed her brother's quiet smile.

Between creating and baking the pastry, allowing it to cool, combining the other ingredients to make the filling and then allowing it all to set in the fridge, it was a full afternoon's event. They moved into the lounge room for a cup of tea while the pie was setting.

"If I'd known how long it'd take, I don't think I would have bothered," Mark said as he sat down.

"Well, you have, Dad, so cheer up! Pie's coming soon!"

"Scrabble, anyone?" Gwen asked.

"Sure!" Samantha said.

"Why not?" Mark said. "Let me whip your butt and put you back in your place."

Gwen found her brother to be an interesting study. He seemed almost scared to enjoy himself and certainly lost with a cup of tea instead of a beer or whisky. She felt an urge to hug him, but there were only so many adjustments he could make in one day. He would probably rush out the door if she did that. She smiled quietly to herself, picturing it.

"What's so funny?" Mark asked, crossing the word "envelope" over her own "evade".

"Nothing, really. Good word."

He nodded.

"Yes, Dad. Good word. Now what on earth am I going to do? You stole my spot!"

The game continued until Gwen's kitchen timer announced the pie would be cooled and ready. As they sat at the kitchen bench on wooden stools, silence settled over them as they savoured their first bite.

Mark was the first to comment. "You've done Mum proud, Gwen."

"Yes, it's divine, but we've *all* done Mum proud, including you, Mark."

"It's delicious!" Samantha agreed.

Gwen's phone pinged with a text message. She ignored it.

"You going to get that?" Mark asked.

She told him it would wait. Gwen knew it would be Russ and was annoyed by the intrusion. The spell was broken, the perfect afternoon shattered by her phone. They each ate a second piece of pie and Mark, a third. While he insisted that she keep the tiny piece that remained, it was half-hearted.

"No, I can make it anytime. You take it, Mark."

"If you don't, Dad, I will!" Samantha threatened.

"OK, OK. I'll take it," he agreed, with laughter. He offered a shy one-armed hug goodbye at the front door, holding the covered plate in his other hand. Gwen returned the hug lightly. She didn't want to break such a fragile soul whose only previous power had been bullying her.

The closed door held her leaning body, supporting her back until they drove away. She stayed there a little longer, resting her head back against it as well. There were no tears, despite the painful joy of how the afternoon had turned out.

❧

Leroy was one of the best-looking clients Gwen had ever

seen. It took all of her focus to greet him warmly and neutrally, as she did with others. She imagined his handsomeness would have been a distraction to others in his life too.

He sat in the purple chair and took a sip of water from the glass she indicated on the side table. He wore an old brown jacket with leather elbow patches, slightly frayed at the collar where his dark curls sat. The tan-coloured trousers looked well worn, a little like his spirit.

"How can I help you today, Leroy?"

It was the sigh she knew: that recognisable sound of a session beginning and someone about to share something terribly vulnerable about themselves with a stranger. She shifted into full listening mode.

"Shit, I don't even know where to start. Oh, sorry. Can I swear here?"

"You can swear as much as you need to. Believe me, these ears have heard every bit of bad language you could think of, and I've probably used some of it myself at times."

He smiled sadly, observing her for the first time, then returning to himself.

"I'm tired, Gwen. I'm beyond that, actually. I'm tired of trying and I'm tired of positive mumbo jumbo, woo-woo stuff that tells me if I just focus my thoughts, my life will change. I've meditated, I've said affirmations, I've written out my goals, made plans, taken action, watched my words, and damn well focused on being grateful. But my life is still shit and, like I said, I'm sick of trying."

"I guess you've done the surrender thing too, then?"

"Yep, you name it. I've read all the books, done the healing, been brave, let go, climbed the mountain, hit the valleys, and I'm still not where I want to be in my life."

"Where do you want to be?"

A tear escaped him. "I just want a regular life, you know – a wife and kids, financial stability. I want to be loved and have someone to love. I don't want to stress over money. I want to enjoy my work. All the usual stuff, really."

"What is the part you're missing the most?"

"A good woman. I'm one of the nice guys, the sort that very few women notice beyond the physical, at least until they're so broken and weary from always choosing bad guys that they rethink things. Then they spend time with someone like me, only to realise they need the drama from the bad guys after all. Surely there must be a woman out there who thinks being treated kindly might actually be a good option."

"Plenty of women like to be treated well, Leroy, but they like growth too. I wonder, do you just aim to please 100 per cent of the time, or are you happy to work through differences?"

"No, I'm happy to voice my opinion," he said. "I'm not a doormat."

They revisited his past, but it was clear he really had done some healing. He had an answer from lived experience for each of her questions.

"Look, Leroy, I know you feel like you've tried everything, but are you open to hope?"

"I do have hope," he said. "And when I lose it, it's never gone for long. But I don't want to always be hoping. I want to be enjoying some progress now."

Gwen guided him to draw a timeline on a large piece of paper that took up most of her desk's top. He wrote down noteworthy events, things in his life that were positive. Standing beside him, occasionally pointing to highlight something, she could smell the earthy scent of his soap. She stood back a little, away from the danger of herself.

When he stood back and looked at the timeline, there was no denying his life *had* actually changed significantly for the better over the years and decades. Much more than he had realised.

"It's easy to wait for the big things in life, Leroy, and to see them as the turning points, the only measure of success. It's also easy to get frustrated when it feels like you're getting nowhere. But life is actually made up of small moments and small steps. The big stuff gets a good rap in movies, and some of it's fabulous in real life too. But it's the little things that carry us forward. There might only be a few big events in a person's life. Do you think you could be giving too much focus to the big things without noticing the huge number of small and lovely things you're achieving and experiencing?"

He considered her perspective. "You're probably right." He looked back to the paper. "Can I keep this?"

"Of course."

He folded it up and returned to sit in the purple chair. Gwen sat in her own chair opposite. She waited to see if he wanted to talk, but he was waiting on her, so she spoke.

"I understand you having those dreams, Leroy. Many people want a mate and to have children, and wanting financial security is a natural thing too. You're closer to that than you know. You eat well. You're paying off a mortgage, even if it's not your dream house yet. You have a good social network, even if you haven't found the right woman."

He nodded. "I know. I really didn't want you to tell me to focus on all that, but you're right. I'd lost track of how many good things I already have in my life."

"Well, we're *all* guilty of trying too hard sometimes, of trying to force life to unfold in certain ways before we're ready. We forget that we're also human beings instead of just human doings and that we don't actually need to find all the answers ourselves. If you've read all the books, then you already have a strong sense of divinity or a higher power. Perhaps you've forgotten it's on your side too. I know I have at times."

"You nailed it when you said I've been trying too hard. Maybe I just need to lighten up and go and have some fun."

"It's a dance, Leroy. Life's a dance, and we all get out of step sometimes by trying to make it all perfect. We forget the fun of simply dancing."

The session finished with a few light jokes, his next appointment scheduled, and a kind farewell.

Two messages came through just as Gwen was finishing up for the day. One was from Russ, asking how her day had gone. This one she ignored. The other was from a guy called Jack.

Hi Gwen. I'm in town and wondered if you're up for that dinner I asked you to once. Free now or soon? It could be fun!

She had met Jack through an old friend soon after her mother died, and declined his invitation for a date as it was too much to think about in her grief.

She re-read the text. *It could be fun!* Yes, she decided. It could be.

An hour later she was sitting by the window in a restaurant facing Jack, the scent of Mediterranean herbs sprinkled over couscous wafting between them. Lively tunes played in the background. She could almost believe she was a young backpacker, traipsing that area all over again. The music was familiar from that chapter of her life, and the food was good.

Jack's company was indeed fun and Gwen found herself laughing easily. As a second glass of red wine slid down her throat, thoughts of Russ slid away with it. It hadn't taken much to feel drunk, since she rarely touched alcohol. When Jack's foot rubbed against her ankle under the table and his eyes spoke of desire, she was too far gone to call a halt. She didn't want to. He reached across the table for her hand. She obliged, and he stroked her fingers. She gulped down the remaining wine in her glass, refilled the glass with her other hand and drank most of that too.

"You may not believe this, Gwen, but I don't usually expect to make love to a woman the first night we're out together. That's the truth, but I'll break that rule tonight if you'll let me."

"All in the name of fun, hey?" she flirted.

"All in the name of fun," he agreed, drawing circles in her palm. "Shall we go?"

Gwen stood up and picked up her handbag. Jack insisted on paying the bill and then opened the restaurant door. She stumbled onto the street outside. Jack caught her before she kissed the footpath.

"Steady now, steady now." Jack's cheery voice echoed in Gwen's ears. She smiled up at him and noticed how delectable his lips seemed in their half-smile.

A familiar voice interrupted them. "Gwen? Gwen?"

She turned around too quickly and almost fell.

"Steady there!" Jack's arm went around her waist.

She didn't hear him. The pain in Russ's eyes as he walked towards them sobered her immediately.

"Gwen! What's going on?"

She couldn't reply. What excuse could she give when it was so obvious?

"Have you been drinking?" He turned to Jack. "How many has she had? She hardly drinks."

"Uh, nearly three large glasses of red wine, I think. Who are you?"

"Who are you is the question, mate. I'm her partner ... and her friend. Who are you?"

Gwen watched the interaction, leaning on Russ for support. Jack shook his head. "No one. Just an old acquaintance who invited Gwen to dinner."

Russ nodded, frowning. "Come on, Gwen. I'll get you home."

She turned to Jack. "Sorry, Jack. I didn't mean—"

"It's cool, Gwen. Dinner was fun."

"Bye," she whispered, looking down, not bothering to watch him walk away. She turned towards Russ instead and opened her mouth to speak, but found no words.

"Come on, Gwen, I'll get you home. Is your bike nearby?" It was still parked out the front of her clinic. "We'll pick it up on the way. It'll fit in my van."

Russ settled Gwen into bed fully clothed, minus her boots. She was asleep before the sound of his van had turned the corner and faded into the distance.

Gwen phoned her first three clients from home and rescheduled their appointments. Unable to reach the fourth, she sighed and got on with the day. At least she had a few hours before that appointment for her headache to ease a little. She drank another large glass of water and made a fruit salad for breakfast. The shower helped but there was no noticing the colours of the day or waving to passing acquaintances when she drove to the clinic.

The purple chair beckoned as she entered. She sat down in it, dropped her handbag at her feet and rested her head against the high back, automatically looking up for the little spider on the chandelier. She was alone without even this small companion to keep her company.

She knew what she wanted, and needed, but those arms were gone forever. Her mother would never hold her again or reassure her that everything would be all right. Whether her mother believed that or not, the positive lie would have pulled her up enough to try and believe it herself.

She kicked off her crimson shoes and tucked her feet under her, leaning into the corner of the chair, trying to feel held.

"Oh, Mum, come back. Please come back," she cried. "Don't be gone. I can't do this alone." She curled up as tight as she could, hiding her face in the cave of her cramped body, and sobbed.

"Uh, hello. Shall I come back later?" Her client had arrived.

Gwen startled and stood quickly. "No, no, I'm sorry. Please, come in. I'll just use the bathroom. I only need a couple of minutes."

"Are you sure?" her client, Bridget, asked. "This really doesn't look like a good time."

"No, it's OK. There's been a death in the family."

"Oh goodness, I'm so sorry."

The client didn't need to know that the death had been nearly two years ago. "Thank you. It's OK, really, it just caught up with me. I'll be here for you in a moment." Gwen rushed down the hallway to the bathroom at the back of the old building, near the lift.

The woman looking back at Gwen from the mirror, even apart from the red eyes, looked like shit. She splashed her face with cold water, ran her fingers through her hair and bounced on her feet. It was a trick she had learnt in qi gong that brought her alive and back to the moment almost immediately. She shook and bounced her whole body, breathing deeply in and out, for another minute, tidied herself one last time, and walked out of the bathroom and down the hallway to her clinic.

The safe, sunny space with its lingering scents from years of delicate candles welcomed her. Healthy green plants in their funky pots set off the purple chair perfectly.

Bridget was standing looking at the flower print on the wall. She turned.

"You look better," she said kindly.

"Yes, it's amazing what some cold water can do," Gwen joked. "I'm sorry you had to be greeted that way, Bridget. May I offer you a cup of tea?" Bridget shook her head. "Then, please," Gwen indicated to the chair, "sit down and tell me how I can help."

Bridget draped her long plait over one shoulder and straightened her perfectly ironed straight grey skirt. "I'm three years short of a dream and I've run out of steam."

"OK," Gwen replied. "What's the dream?"

"To retire at 55 and learn to draw properly. Then spend my days sketching whatever scene is in front of me. I used to love drawing when I was a child and teenager. I'm 52 now, a human resources manager who hasn't drawn for years, and I don't know if I can keep going for another three years."

Gwen asked her why she absolutely had to wait that long. Was it a financial decision?

"Not really, though another three years' wages would set me up very differently. No, it's because I've set a goal of 55 and I've never quit on a plan before."

"So you like things always to be predictable?"

"That's ... very direct." Bridget seemed offended.

Gwen smiled gently. "I wouldn't have said it if I didn't think you could handle it." Bridget's agitation lessened so Gwen continued. "Sorry. Let me put it another way. Have all your plans turned out exactly as you intended? Hasn't life thrown a few curve balls into the mix sometimes, and you've survived it?"

"Well, yes, of course. But this is something I can control."

"Even if you're already exhausted from trying to, by staying in a job longer than your heart wants?"

Bridget said she would feel like she had failed if she didn't stick with her plan. As they dived deeper, looking honestly at some of her beliefs, Bridget admitted to using that as an excuse, to cover being scared to act on what she wanted.

Gwen reminded her of the sacredness of her time, that she didn't have forever, and asked if she really wanted to put her long-held dream on hold for another three years.

"You know what? I don't. It's so liberating admitting that. Which means I need a new plan. I need to set a date to leave."

Gwen smiled.

"OK, then. Is there anything that could help you decide on a particular date?"

Bridget looked away pondering and then smiled.

"Oh goodness! There's this week-long drawing retreat that's held every year. I've always wanted to go. I was planning for that to be the first indulgence once I retired, but this year's retreat is two months away. Maybe I could line my resignation up with that. What do you think?"

"I think it would be a very fine welcome into your new life."

Bridget's smile continued to expand.

"Oh, my goodness!" She stamped her feet up and down in excitement. "I'm doing it! I'm really going to do this!"

Gwen laughed, grateful for the reminder of how much joy serving others could bring. "Yes, because you're a brave and amazing woman."

"Thanks, Gwen. You're right. I was just scared." Bridget beamed as tears of joy surfaced.

After they had said goodbye and the door had closed, Gwen sat in the purple chair, hearing her own words. *Time is sacred. You don't have forever.* Did she want to put her own dreams on hold by using excuses and staying with the stale old stories about the glories of independence? With a heavy heart for the previous night's behaviour, she realised Russ was part of a dream she hadn't known she longed for.

Gwen had thought she was being ghosted by Russ once before, but that time he had actually been in hospital. This time, he was indeed ghosting her. She had tried to reach him three times, with the only consolation of his refusal to answer being the sound of his voice in the message before she apologised each time. She could only say sorry so many times. Any path forward needed an honest conversation in person, but she had to respect his decision. Gwen didn't blame him. She had pushed his tender heart away many more times than she had encouraged him.

Tuesday afternoons, once her favourite time of the week, lost their shine. Driving to unknown destinations, the same. Instead, Gwen visited places of shared memories: the pub where she and Russ had enjoyed their first lunch, the car park of their first kiss, the creek they had gone to for a picnic and had made out until her face was raw from kissing. She even parked outside the hospital where she had visited him after his accident. When she found herself driving a few hours to the coast just to stay at the resort where they had watched whales migrating, she knew she was in trouble.

It wasn't ego that was stopping her from letting him go; it wasn't ego behind her refusal to hear the rejection implicit in his lack of contact. It was that he was the loveliest, kindest man she had ever met. He was her dear friend and the man she was ready to love. Only now she had lost him.

One afternoon, she parked a little up the street from his newsagency. She caught a glimpse of him in his store, laughing with a customer. The woman walked out smiling and Gwen's heart dropped. Had he already moved on? She couldn't blame him if he had. She turned the car key and drove off before he could see her.

It was time to let go.

Her own tender heart took her to the cemetery later that day. Her mother's tombstone was cold against her side as she sat on the grass, unconsciously stroking the place where her mother's face might be. Tears mingled with her silent questions. *How can I still be alive when I feel so much pain? How does a heart keep beating when it is broken?*

She took a deep breath through her tears but the questions continued. *How can I keep supporting others when there is nothing left to lift me? If I'm not supporting others, though, what would be left? Nothing.*

She decided that if she couldn't keep going for herself, she would at least do so for her mother.

"Thanks, Mum," Gwen said with a soft smile, patting the grass. "You always know the answers. I'll do it for you until I can do it for myself again."

She didn't notice the person she walked past on the way back to the car, but he noticed her. "Gwen?"

Her bleary eyes looked into the handsome eyes of Jack.

"Jack."

"I won't ask if you're OK, since we're at a cemetery. I have to ask if you're OK with your fella, though. I didn't mean to step on any toes there."

"I could have said no to your invitation, Jack, but I didn't."

"So you sorted it out?"

Gwen frowned and took a breath. "No, actually, we didn't."

Jack didn't reply, just looked kindly at her. "Gwen, would you like to go for a coffee, just as friends? It looks like you could do with some company."

"You know, Jack, you're right. I could do with some company, but I'm going to decline your kind invitation, as tempting as it is."

He nodded. "Well, you take care then, Gwen."

She thanked him and wished him the same, then walked back to her car. Once in the driver's seat, with some hesitation, she phoned her brother Mark. Neither had ever reached out to the other when in need. She could have phoned Samantha, or even her younger sister, Petra, who was acting a lot more human and caring these days. It was strong arms she needed, though, even if she and Mark had hardly hugged in their life.

He answered on the second ring. "Gwen! This is a surprise. Are you OK?"

"Not really. I could do with a hug."

"Where are you?"

"At the cemetery. Can you come?"

"Sure. I can be there in about 15 minutes. Can you hang in there until then?"

Through her tears, she replied that she could.

"Gwen?" he asked, just before she hung up.

"Yes?"

"Thanks for reaching out."

Her tears prevented her from replying as she hung up and walked back to her mother.

Being held, with no agenda or judgment, did more for Gwen than any conversation could have. Mark's large frame held her safely, his chin resting gently on her head. She felt his own body shake with tears. Gwen had no idea how long they stood by their mother's grave. All she knew was that years of animosity and misunderstandings fell away with their tears.

They walked back to the parking area, her arm linked through her brother's. So many tears had left her exhausted.

The white van was like any other, except it wasn't. Russ pulled into the car park, the only space available right in front of where she and Mark stood to say goodbye.

"Oh, God," Gwen whispered. Mark looked from her to Russ, who was getting out of the car.

"Gwen. Hi," Russ said with hesitancy, and then looked from her to Mark.

"Hi, Russ. This is my brother, Mark. Mark, this is Russ ..." She had no idea how to explain their connection.

"A friend," he said to Mark, reaching out and shaking his hand.

The men exchanged pleasantries, then Mark said he needed to get home to the family. He kissed Gwen's forehead. "See you soon, sis," he smiled. With a heart raw, open and exhausted, she nodded.

Gwen and Russ watched him walk off. She was too drained to say much so turned and simply said, "I'm sorry."

Russ met her gaze. "I could do with some honesty from you, Gwen."

"It's obvious, isn't it? I got scared."

"And you don't think I was? Shit, I've buried my wife and child. I wasn't a horny 16-year-old who'd jump at any opportunity."

"I know, Russ. I'm sorry. It was easy being with you at first, then I started feeling suffocated. I'm an independent woman. I like the freedom of spontaneity, of not telling someone every single day what I've been up to. I have to keep some of me for me."

"Gwen, I said I wanted a relationship with you. I didn't say I wanted to *change* you. With all your insight into human behaviour, had it not occurred to you that I found your independence attractive? That I liked the mystery of you? I have my own life too, you know."

Gwen looked at his shoes. Good quality. Trendy in a country sort of way.

"Gwen, look at me," he said. Her eyes rose to his. "I was

always willing to build foundations first. You can't have a fairy tale without a beginning, but you were already running from the middle long before we got there. I thought we had something special, or the potential of it at least, but there had to be trust."

She nodded and gulped down her pain as he continued. "Seeing you with that bloke that night was such a shock. Even worse than that was seeing you drunk and on self-destruct, when all we needed to do was talk about it as adults. Isn't that your job, helping people talk their hard stuff out? And you can't even do it yourself?"

"Well, yes," she admitted. "But don't plumbers have leaky taps at home? Not everyone who works in mental health has it sorted, you know."

"Gwen." His hands rose and rested on her upper arms. "You're a beautiful, messed-up, quirky, brilliant, sexy woman. I'm not looking for perfection. I'm far from it myself! I'm looking for you, as you are. That's it. Don't you want to come on the ride with me and have an adventure?"

Tears poured from her eyes without restraint. "Are you saying you'd still have me? After this?"

"Well, life has put us in front of each other yet again, hasn't it? Maybe it's trying to tell us something." He touched the side of her face tenderly. "Of course I'd still have you, but only if you're willing to be brave."

A sob burst from her.

"Come here," he whispered, wrapping his arms around her. She leant into him, her tears wetting the shoulder of his shirt until there were none left. He lifted her chin with one finger and kissed her.

"Mmm," she murmured. "How can a kiss, a simple touching of the lips, be so magnificent? How can a heart break and heal all in one day? How can one cry and laugh in the same minute?"

He silenced her with kisses.

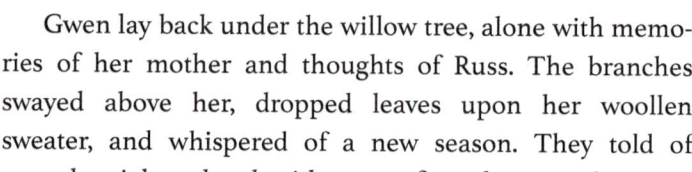

Gwen lay back under the willow tree, alone with memories of her mother and thoughts of Russ. The branches swayed above her, dropped leaves upon her woollen sweater, and whispered of a new season. They told of snuggly nights ahead with warm fires, homemade soups and toes entwined under flannelette sheets.

When the warmth of the sun hinted at fading, she rose and brushed the yellow leaves from her backside, looked down one last time to the meandering river, and then picked up her bike and climbed on. The soft light of the autumn afternoon accompanied her home.

ABOUT THE AUTHOR

Bronnie Ware is the author of the international bestselling memoir *The Top Five Regrets of the Dying*, published in 32 languages, with a movie in the pipeline.

She is a TEDx speaker and has been interviewed by Wall St Journal, ABC Radio National, The Guardian, The Sunday Times, Harvard Business Review, and hundreds of publications worldwide.

She has also been interviewed on numerous podcasts including by Dr Wayne Dyer, Marie Forleo, Fearne Cotton, Lewis Howes, Dr Rangan Chatterjee, and Tami Simon.

Bronnie lives in rural Australia and is a respected teacher of courage on the global stage. She is an advocate for simplicity and leaving space to breathe, drawing on courage to follow the heart and allow life to provide the shortcuts.

To find out more about Bronnie's teachings, visit bron nieware.com

ALSO BY BRONNIE WARE

The Top Five Regrets of the Dying: A Life Transformed by the Dearly Departing

Your Year for Change: 52 Reflections for Regret-Free Living

Bloom: A Tale of Courage, Surrender, and Breaking Through Upper Limits

From 25 Rejections to a Million Readers: Essential Tips for Budding Authors

The Purple Chair: An inspirational, short-story, fiction series celebrating the fragility and strength of being human

The Top Five Regrets of the Dying - Digital Card Deck

Inspirational Prints to enhance your home

Read more from Bronnie at bronnieware.com